I0719284

The Ghosts
of
Ynys Enlli

This work of fiction is the product of the author's imagination. Any resemblance to persons living or dead is entirely coincidental.

Coypright © 2025 by John W. Conlee

All rights reserved. This book, or parts thereof, may not be reproduced without written permission. Published in the United States by Pale Horse Books.

ISBN: 978-1-939917-40-9

Cover Design: Sally Stiles

www.PaleHorseBooks.com

Also by John Conlee:

    THE DRAGON STONE
    A CUP OF KINDNESS
    THE KING OF MUD & GRASS
    IN THE SUMMER COUNTRY
    THE HEATER
    ROUNDING THIRD
    THE VOYAGE OF MAELDUN
    THE BROTHERS PENDRAGON
    THE LAST PENDRAGON
    CATACLYSM
    THE CHAUCER CODEX
    THE LANCE OF LONGINUS
    THE RAREST BOOK IN THE WORLD

The Ghosts
of
Ynys Enlli

John Conlee

Pale Horse Books

AUTHOR'S NOTE

This novel, like many works of fiction, blends the real with the imaginary. Ynys Enlli—in English, Bardsey Island—is a real island off the tip of the Llŷn Peninsula in North Wales. For many centuries since the early Middle Ages, it has been a place of pilgrimage for devout Christians. It is likely, in fact, to have been a holy site in pre-Christian times. While some monastic ruins still survive on the island, they are not nearly as extensive or as well-preserved as here depicted. Nor is there an active brotherhood of monks on the island. The Bardsey apple tree, however, does exist and is as enigmatic as described in the story.

Several of the major characters in this novel have been borrowed from Sir Arthur Conan Doyle's Professor Challenger novels and tales, in particular Professor George Edward Challenger, his close friend Lord John Roxton, and his son-in-law, Ted Malone.

Far and away the most important of Conan Doyle's Professor Challenger works is the novel *The Lost World*. The depictions of Doyle's characters here, one hopes, are not greatly inconsistent with how they are portrayed in that novel or in Doyle's other works.

"· · · · ·

The spirit-world around this world of sense
Floats like an atmosphere, and everywhere
Wafts through these earthly mists and vapours dense
A vital breath of more ethereal air.

Our little lives are kept in equipoise
By opposite attractions and desires;
The struggle of the instinct that enjoys,
And the more noble instinct that aspires.
· · · · · ·

And as the moon from some dark cloud
Throws o'er the sea a floating bridge of light,
Across those trembling planks our fancies crowd
Into the realm of mist and night,—

So from the world of spirits there descends
A bridge of light, connecting it with this,
O'er whose unsteady floor, that sways and bends,
Wander our thoughts above the dark abyss.
· · · · · "

— verses taken from "Haunted Houses," **H. W. Longfellow**

1

The thick fog enshrouding the streets near Victoria Station slowed my journey, and by the time I arrived at Professor Challenger's third-floor flat in Victoria Gardens, all the others were there. Near the coal fire that glowed behind the grate, four men sat ensconced in comfortable chairs in a semi-circle around my father-in-law, Professor George Edward Challenger. The professor looked up and gave me an acknowledging nod as I slipped out of my coat and lowered myself on the one remaining empty chair.

"*Ghosts?*" a man I didn't know offered in a tremulous voice. "Are you talking about *ghosts?*"

"More what I prefer to call psychic manifestations," replied Dr. Nathaniel Atkinson, the famous surgeon from St. Mary's Hospital. The other three men maintained a thoughtful silence.

"Perhaps we should tell Ted what this is all about," said

Lord John Roxton. I'd come to know Lord Roxton well more than ten years ago, when he and I, along with Professor Challenger and Professor Summerlee, now deceased, had journeyed together up the Amazon River in South America. It was on that trip that the four of us had proved once and for all that Professor Challenger's 'Lost World' truly existed.

"I'm afraid I was the one who started this hare by reporting a rumor I had heard," said the Reverend Charles Mason, a man I knew only slightly. "The others took it from there." He shrugged and gave me an apologetic look. I knew that the Reverend J. M. Mason, a smallish, dapper man with a neat goatee, was currently making a name for himself in London's Methodist circles.

"But, ghosts?" the man named Wilkins said again.

"Ted," said Professor Challenger, "this fellow is McCauley Wilkins. I'm told he's something big in the London financial world."

"Hello, sir," I said, reaching out a hand. "I'm Ted Malone."

"Pleasure, Mr. Malone," the man said, deigning to offer me a limpish handshake. He was a small and slightly chubby-looking fellow wearing a three-piece suit with a mauve ascot atop his crisp white shirt.

"Now, Wilkins," said my father-in-law, returning to the conversation my entrance had interrupted, "these ghosts they are talking about are not desiccated old women in long white gowns carrying candles along third-floor hallways in an ancient country house. That's not the type of ghost they have in mind." His tone of voice sounded a little disdainful.

"Then please enlighten me, sir, if you'd be so kind," Wilkins replied.

"I shall leave that to Mason or Atkinson," Challenger said. "They are the true believers here, not I."

"Quite right," Dr. Atkinson said "We're not talking ghosts as popularly portrayed in tales, or more recently, in the cinema. I think I can best illustrate the kind of thing I mean by relating a personal anecdote."

"Then go right ahead," Wilkins said.

"A couple of years ago, sir, I was traveling with friends in Scotland. We had stopped off for a brief visit at that infamous site known as Glencoe, since it was on our route back to Edinburgh. As we wandered about, a terrible sense of oppression suddenly came upon me. It was a largely indefinable feeling, though I felt as if I was being crushed by it. It was like nothing I had ever experienced before. It was as if I were being enveloped by evil. Strangely, none of my companions seemed to share it. The feeling grew so strongly terrifying to me that I insisted we depart immediately from that horrible place."

"Glencoe—where the Campbells treacherously set upon the MacDonalds, murdering them by night?" I asked.

"That's the very place," Challenger said, "where occurred one of the most heinous events in the history of the Highland clans."

"So," Wilkins said, "you began to see the murdered ghosts

of the McDonalds?"

"No, no. I saw no ghosts," Dr. Atkinson replied. "It's what I felt that's of the utmost importance. What came upon me was a powerful, oppressive sense of being in the presence of evil. It felt palpable. I was enveloped by it. I had to get away from that vile place, and I couldn't do it fast enough."

" 'By the pricking of my thumbs,' " intoned the professor, "something wicked this way comes.' "

"Yes. But it wasn't just my thumbs that felt it," Dr. Atkinson said. "I felt that wickedness suffuse my whole being. Anyway, my companions, confused by my behavior but knowing that I was in the throes of some great torment, acquiesced to my desire, and we soon continued on our way. Once we'd put some distance between us and Glencoe my emotional equilibrium returned. After that it was as if nothing untoward had happened. But the feeling of it remains with me to this day."

"But what had happened?" Wilkins asked.

"It's my guess that I had a psychic experience of the worst kind. Somehow, I had tapped into the spiritual residue of the powerful emotions generated by the actions of the Campbells and the McDonalds that night, the psychic remnants of hatred and intense fear."

"What he's suggesting," Challenger offered, "is the theory that people in the throes of powerful emotions—particularly powerful negative ones—project those psychic experiences into the space about them and that those emotions can remain trapped there. Then, later on, it's possible for innocent bystanders to stumble upon them—as seems to have happened to our worthy friend."

"Like wandering into a place where there's a pocket of bad karma?" the Reverend Mason said.

"If you wish, yes."

"But what about the others? Why didn't they feel what you felt?" Wilkins asked.

Dr. Atkinson tilted his head and gave a one-shoulder shrug. "I can't say for certain, but I think it may be a matter of variable receptivity. Call it being on the right wavelength, if you prefer. This was the only time in my life when I've had such an experience. I must surely have come across places on other occasions where such energy persists yet on those occasions I didn't feel a thing. I wasn't on the right wavelength.

"I have been to the great battlefields at the Somme and Passchendaele, and while I felt heartsick in the knowledge of what happened there, I had no experience comparable to what I felt at Glencoe. At those terrible battlefields there must have been vast stores of emotional residue, but I felt none of it. My receptors weren't in tune with it. My surmise is that some people respond to certain kinds of psychic experiences and not to others. Perhaps the fact of the matter is that some people are completely tone deaf to all varieties of residual emotions, just as some people are colorblind and others are tone deaf and have no sense of musical pitch."

"I must be one of those," Wilkins said. "I've had no experiences like the one you describe at Glencoe."

"Well, I have," I said. "In the Amazon on the high plateau with all the ancient creatures. Professor Challenger will remember."

"I remember how frightened you were, but I assumed—and still assume—it was understandable terror at the sight of all those ape-men attacking us."

"I was frightened by the sight of those monstrous beings," I replied, "but it was more than that. It was as if some long-nascent experience had suddenly come over me. What I was feeling wasn't something new to me; it was as if I had felt it before, eons earlier. A kind of déjà-vu feeling."

"Ah, paramnesia," said Challenger.

"I, too, have had such experiences," Lord Roxton said, his light-blue eyes staring not at the other men but into the fire, "on almost all of my adventures." There was a wistfulness to his voice.

"Have any of you ever heard of a place called Ynys Enlli?" the Reverend Mason asked.

"Are you referring to the holy islet off the coast of Wales?" the professor asked.

"Yes, that's the one I mean. It's reputed to be one of the places where the veil between the spirit world and our world can most readily be pierced."

The man named Wilkins suddenly leapt to his feet. "This has all been most fascinating," he blurted, "but I'm afraid I must be on my way just now. I would enjoy a continuation of this fascinating topic." Looking nervous, he slipped into his coat and rushed from the flat.

"Fascinating topic indeed," scoffed Professor Challenger. "I say that everything you chaps have just been spouting is absolute bosh. Bosh, pure and simple."

2

I stayed behind after the others had departed to have a more intimate visit with my father-in-law. It had been the better part of a month since I'd had a chance to do that, since I had been off in the wilds of Scotland on assignment for my newspaper, *The Daily Gazette.* And now, as I studied him carefully, I found his appearance quite shocking. Both his immense physical bulk and his massive vitality seemed greatly diminished. They seemed to have been reduced nearly to the level of most ordinary mortals—and there had never been anything ordinary about Professor Challenger. Now there was a droop to his powerfully muscled shoulders, and even his huge, bearded head seemed to have shrunk perceptibly. His irascibility was still quite present, though his loud, growling voice seemed uncharacteristically subdued.

"I've missed you, Ted," he said, with genuine emotion.

"You and Roxton are about the only friends I have left. And, as you know, John can be an aloof so-and-so." I spotted a tight smile upon his lips through his tangled beard, a beard once jet-black but now shot through with gray.

I found his remarks ironic since that was how most people, with good reason, found my father-in-law's behavior. It was only toward his wife and daughter that he had ever manifested any warmth or sentimentality. Now, tragically, they were both gone. And I shared his grief. For his daughter, Enid, had been my wife for the happiest two years of my life. It was now just over a year since she'd died in London's great tram disaster: A lorry collided with the tram car she was on, killing her and another passenger. In that same year her mother Jessica, long the apple of the professor's eye, had fallen victim to the Spanish flu, along with thousands of others.

The great man's somewhat shrunken appearance, no doubt, was the consequence of his double sorrow. I felt sure that he experienced his grief, like he experienced everything else, at a superhuman level. My own pain at losing Enid was excruciating, and I knew that losing both Enid and Jessie must have been close to unbearable for him. I had lost my dearest friend and companion; he had lost the two human beings who were the supreme joys of his existence and who gave him reason to live.

"Sir, who was that chap who departed so suddenly?"

"Wilkins? Just some friend of the Reverend Mason. Said

to be a notable figure in London financial circles. Quite a bore, you ask me. Wilkins. McCauley Wilkins."

"Ah. I have heard of the bloke."

At that moment Austin, the professor's long-time manservant, stepped through the door to the small dining room. Austin was a dried-up fellow of uncertain age. Using both hands, he bore a round wooden tray on which sat two small glasses half filled with an amber liquid.

He stepped over to me and held the tray poised before me. "Evening, Mr. Malone," he said. "The master thought you might like to have a little sip of something from your native nation."

I smiled at that remark. Challenger knew I had developed a preference for Irish whisky, a fact which never ceased to amuse my father-in-law. He must have anticipated that I would remain behind for a little chat. The man had a knack for always being one step ahead of everyone else.

"Thank you, Austin," I said. "Most kind." He dipped his head in acknowledgment. Then, after offering the other glass to the professor, he retreated from the room.

"Good old Austin," I said, raising my glass. "To my native nation." I was, in fact, Irish by birth, though I was a Londoner through and through, my parents having come over to find work when I was just a wee lad.

"Now, more than ever, I would be lost without Austin," the professor said with a sigh. And then after a long pause he said, "So, Ynys Enlli. Ever heard of it before tonight?"

"Sorry, no. It's a place that's managed to escape my notice."

"Then perhaps we should correct that lacuna?"

"Meaning what, sir?"

"Ted, I'm going crazy sitting here stewing in self-pity. We need an adventure, my lad. You must talk that editor of yours into giving you an assignment to look into ghosts. Roxton would surely join us. It would be like old times. Too bad we don't have old Summerlee to add his caustic cynicism to our endeavor. But my own cynicism might well prove sufficiently ample."

3

Standing on the *Embankment, McCauley Wilkins stared down at the brown, oily water of the River Thames. Here, in the center of London, he had never found the Thames a particularly attractive river, not like the Rhine as it flowed through the heart of Cologne or the Danube as it bisected Buda and Pest. Upriver the Thames might be far more attractive, perhaps the stretch from Henley to Oxford, but here it definitely was not—not today, not to the eyes of McCauley Wilkins. Or was he merely casting about for a rationalization not to do what he had come to do?*

The Reverend Charles Mason, on whom Wilkins had been counting, had offered him faint consolation. But when it came right down to it, Wilkins knew that he was too much of a coward to leap into the river and put an end to all his grief. Suicide was the coward's way out; but McCauley Wilkins was too cowardly even to be such a coward. "That one more river to cross" was the time-honored phrase, but today the Thames would not be that river, not for Mr. McCauley Wilkins.

Ghosts. The men last night had talked of ghosts—or spiritual emanations or manifestations or some such thing. It had sounded like gibberish to him, and yet all that talk of ghosts had terrified him. Could there be something to it? How he wished Dr. Atkinson and the Reverend Mason might help him find solace. Should he go with these men to this far-off Island in Wales? It might be worth the attempt. If it led nowhere, he would be no worse off than he already was, would he? And if he were, there was always the river.

Last night McCauley Wilkins had denied that he'd ever had an experience like the one Dr. Atkinson described having at Glencoe. But the truth was, he had.

4

"So, Mr. Ted Malone," McArdle said to me as I stepped into the newspaper editor's office, "you've finally decided to grace us with your presence and return from the wilds of my beloved Scotland, have you? Well, my lad, I hope you'll be havin' something to show for your month's employment or enjoyment." McArdle looked exactly as he always had—scraggily bearded face, receding reddish hair, rounded shoulders, a slight paunch at his waist.

"I did enjoy my outing, sir, and I do have something to show for it." I handed him the sheets I'd spent several hours typing up last night. "I think they will be to your liking, and more importantly, to the liking of our readers."

Since the sensation I had created several years ago with the serial correspondence I'd sent from South America concerning the Lost World, I had made quite a name for myself in London journalistic circles, and I had pretty much single-handedly taken *The News Gazette* from being a minor London daily to one of the city's most widely read rags, if I do say so myself. As a consequence of that early success, I had often been given my head to go charging off hither and yon in pursuit of stories to excite our readers. My track record with such pursuits was excellent, a combination of good luck and good judgment, though I will admit my good judgment often came from following the advice of Professor Summerlee, Lord John Roxton, and most especially, Professor George Edward Challenger.

"So, Ted," Mr. McArdle said, "you'll be settlin' down here in foggy old London Town for a good bit now, eh laddie?"

"Well, actually sir, something came up last night that I think may interest you. I feel certain it will interest our readers."

McArdle's pale blue eyes beneath his shaggy reddish eyebrows squinted at me. "Already? You've hardly been back a single day."

"I'll confess, sir, that I spent some time last night with Professor Challenger."

"Oh, dear me. So, Malone, what's it going to be this time, eh?"

"It's ghosts, sir. This time it's ghosts."

"Good Lord—*ghosts.*"

Austin, my father-in-law's manservant, welcomed me at the door and ushered me into the familiar flat. I saw no sign of the professor, but as Austin placed my coat on the coat rack, I noticed that Lord Roxton's hat and coat were already there. Then I caught the murmur of low voices coming from the professor's study.

I waited patiently in the sitting room until the two men appeared. "Ah, Ted, good of you to come," Challenger said in an unusually affable voice.

"I heard a rumor that you'd brought in the chef from Fabricio's for tonight's meal," I said, "so I could hardly stay away."

"I thought we should treat ourselves to a proper meal before we go trekking to the far-off wilds of Wales." John Roxton smiled at the professor's words.

"Well, sir, it's not exactly as if we were going up the Amazon River again," I said. "The Welsh are well known for their sheep but not for their triceratops."

"And also for their rabbits," the professor said, making a feeble joke about the fondness of the Welsh for the dish Welsh rarebit.

"Who else is coming tonight?" I asked.

"Everyone is coming. Tonight it's Uncle Tom Cobley and all."

"The reverend and the doctor?"

"Oh, yes. And that business chap as well. I didn't much want the fellow to be in on our adventure, but Mason insisted. Thinks it may help the blighter with some problem he has."

I was hoping it might help Professor Challenger with his problem, too, but I remained mum on that point.

"Evening, Austin," I said, as the manservant came in balancing a large tray.

"Sherry, sir?" I reached for the delicate glass and nodded my thanks.

A moment later the other three men arrived in a group. Animated conversation soon filled the room. The only ones who remained on the sidelines were me and the man named Wilkins. Professor Challenger, as was his wont, enjoyed carrying the ball into the midst of the scrum.

"Roxton and I were just looking at the map and studying the best routes to get us there," he said. "We can go a good bit of the way by rail. I suggest we break our journey thrice, first at Chester, then at Bangor, and then perhaps on our third night we'll pause in Pwllheli. From there we'll probably need to procure a horse-drawn conveyance to carry us out to Aberdaron at the tip end of the peninsula—unless you'd prefer to walk it."

"If we're passing ourselves off as pilgrims, I think we should walk," I said.

"Then we hire a fisherman or someone to take us out to the island by boat?" asked Dr. Atkinson.

"Yes," said Mason, "but how soon we can do that will depend on the weather. It's a short crossing but a most treacherous stretch of water. Requires a calm day, a calm sea, and a calm hand at the tiller."

"So, if all goes to plan," Wilkins said, finally speaking up, "it should take us four or five days to get there? That seems rather a long time for such a short journey."

"You are right, it's not a vast distance," Lord Roxton said, "but it's a very remote place. In many areas Wales is still a quite primitive land, and this is one of them. Modes of transport there have hardly changed since the Middle Ages."

"If you don't have a couple of weeks to spare for this adventure," Challenger said, "then perhaps you shouldn't come."

"No, no," Wilkins bleated, "I'm definitely in."

The Reverend Mason, who was seated next to Wilkins, reached out and patted his arm reassuringly. The two men obviously had a close relationship. That was a good thing, I thought, because it seemed to me that none of the rest of us were so keen on Mr. Wilkins. Especially not Professor Challenger.

Our dinner was splendid. The wine flowed and so did the conversation. And to my relief, not a single word was spoken about ghosts.

The plan that emerged was for us to set off by rail eight days hence, leaving from London's Euston Station. Lord Roxton said—and Mason and Atkinson both concurred— that it was essential that we be out on Ynys Enlli a day or two before the beginning of May. Something to do with the ancient Celtic calendar, apparently. That was a subject

I decided I should swot up on in the few days before our departure.

5

My editor, Mr. McArdle, seemed pleased with my piece on Scotland, though he corrected my spelling in several places, especially concerning Scottish place names. He only axed a few paragraphs, ones he deemed superfluous. I disagreed, but he's the editor.

"Sir," I said, "how's your knowledge of the ancient Celtic calendar?"

"Better than most. What would ya like to be knowing, laddie?"

"For one thing, what's so special about the beginning of May?"

"O, laddie, ya don't be knowing *that?* For shame, my boy, and you have an Irish name, too. You're an embarrassment to your Celtic heritage, Ted Malone."

"Sir, I may have Irish parents and an Irish surname, but I was raised a Londoner and I'm proud of it."

"But beneath that London patina, Ted, you've kept your Irish temperament. Ya cannae be denying that, my lad."

"That's what Challenger has told me on many occasions. But sir, back to the merry month of May. What's so special about it?"

"I'll make it simple for your simple Irish brain. The year consists of two six-month halves, right?"

"If you say so."

"The winter half begins on the first of November."

"All Saints' Day."

"The Celts called it Samhain, but aye, All Saints' Day. Anyway, the summer half of the year begins on May Day. The Celts called it Beltane."

"Okay, yes, I've heard of that."

"Those are the two most important dates. The first of February, Imbolc, and the first of August, Lughnasa, are important also, but maybe a bit less so. So, May 1st and November 1st are the big ones."

"But what makes them so special?"

"Ah, well, the ancient Celts believed that where the two halves of the year connect, there's a seam. The old folks always claimed that at midnight on Halloween and again on May Day Eve it was possible for the spirits to slip through. Apparently, that's also the time that faerie abductions sometimes occurred. But, my laddie, I suggest you consult the learned authorities. Maybe you need to spend a few hours in Dr. Williams's famous library and bone up on the subject."

I nodded. "I'll try to do that. Oh, and sir, do you know anything about a chap called McCauley Wilkins? He seems to be a big noise in London financial circles."

"So where have you been, my lad? Oh yes, Scotland. So p'haps that's why you're so benighted. That fella ya just named, why that cove was much in the news about five weeks ago."

"Fill me in, sir."

"Coppers thought he'd murdered his wife. It was splashed all over the front page of most of the papers, though not ours. We took the cautious approach. Good thing, too, because a day or two later they concluded he was perfectly innocent. He'd been able to prove he'd been in Bristol at the time of her death, which they placed between 12 and 3 in the morning. Died from a letter-opener stab wound to the heart. Wilkins was in Bristol for a business meeting, and at the time of her death he was in a card game with three others over a hundred miles away.

"Wilkins discovered her body the next day when he returned in the early afternoon. She was lying sprawled out on her back in the middle of the carpet, the handle of the letter-opener planted deep in her chest pointing toward the ceiling."

"Goodness," I said.

"Police concluded it was a crime of passion. There were two nearly empty wine glasses on the small table in the room, and the woman was dishabille. A lovers' tryst gone wrong, to all appearances. No one has been arrested, and the police remain tight-lipped about it. In a day or two the scandal rags moved on to other stories, and the whole thing slipped from public attention. Anyway, why this interest in McCauley Wilkins?"

"I met the chap the other night at Professor Challenger's flat. I found him a rather colorless fella, but I got the feeling he was on edge about something. Now I can see why."

The following day I acted upon McCardle's suggestion and went to Dr. Williams's library. After spending three hours there I felt I'd become a minor expert on the Celtic Holy Days. I'd learned quite a lot about them. Maybe I now knew nearly as much about them as Professor Challenger surely knew.

6

McCauley Wilkins *slipped through the entryway to the Temple Church and slumped down on a nearby pew. The remarkable little church tucked away in the heart of London's law courts and legal chambers was nearly empty. A few folks wandered about in the nave section where all the stone effigies were laid out on the floor, the most famous of them being the one of the great twelfth-century hero William the Marshall, the champion of Henry II.*

Wilkins often came here on his midday break. There was a special serenity in the dark little church, and on most days the church organist came to practice between one and two. The man usually played well-known pieces by Bach and Handel, though, like McCauley Wilkins, he was also partial to the English composers Purcell and Tillis. Now and then he would play something more modern, but Wilkins preferred the earlier composers.

Today, after working through pieces by several composers, the organist suddenly broke into the opening bars of Richard Strauss's Also Sprach Zarathustra. *The dramatic beginning of the work was a shock to McCauley's system. Grand and glorious music, to be sure, but not the gentle soul-soothing music of Thomas Tillis that Wilkins had been looking forward to hearing. Still, as he listened, the music began to grow on him. Could Zarathustra have something to say to him? Something he needed to hear?*

When the organist had concluded the initial fanfare section to the tone poem, he stopped playing and paused for fully half a minute. Wilkins concluded that the man's practice session was over, and he was preparing to leave when the organist began playing Bach's "Jesu Joy of Man's Desiring." As the ethereal music washed over him, McCauley Wilkins found himself slipping into a waking reverie.

He saw himself standing in the sitting room of his London flat. Then he saw that Felicity, his wife, had entered the room. She was dressed for a night out on the town. She looked marvelous in a green satin evening gown, her hair arranged in a side-swept finger wave, a style he hadn't seen her wear before. McCauley knew it wasn't for him she'd taken such pains. He didn't know who it was for, but he knew it wasn't for him. "You needn't wait up," she said. "I have my key."

McCauley suddenly realized that in his right hand he held his old Webley service revolver.

Seeing the pistol, Felicity said with a smirk, "A gun? Oh my, oh my."

"My old army revolver," he said.

"Some soldier you were," she scoffed, "but I guess even the army needed its accountants."

Felicity was a woman McCauley had loved. And the truth was he still did. But she had grown cold, for he was just a boring, middle-aged banker who'd lost his vigor and his youthful good looks.

"Felicity, don't go," he said in a pleading voice.

"You were once so promising," she said.

He cocked the pistol and pointed it at her.

"I'll see you in hell before you have the guts to pull that trigger," she said.

McCauley's anger was palpable. She had humiliated him once too often. He felt his finger pressing against the revolver's trigger.

A loud noise roused McCauley Wilkins from his reverie. Someone on a nearby pew must have dropped a hymnal or something. Slowly it came to him that he was still sitting in the Temple Church and that the organist was still playing soft music.

What McCauley had just experienced in his reverie intensified his feelings of despair. He dropped down onto the kneeler before him, his hands to his face, and he began to sob.

"Felicity, I am sorry," he finally managed to whisper. "I am so very sorry."

7

I spent my evening hours the following week familiarizing myself with the supernatural by means of the tales of M.R. James and Algernon Blackwood. Creepy, frightening yarns, most of them, but nothing more than the products of the authors' strange imaginations. At least, that's what I told myself. Nothing to put any stock in. I also read Henry James's *The Turn of the Screw* and re-read Oscar Wilde's *The Picture of Dorian Gray.*

Two days before our scheduled departure I managed to entice Professor Challenger to emerge from his abode by inviting him to join me for lunch at a small restaurant that I knew he liked near Covent Garden. After we settled in at our table and made our orders, I began telling him what I'd been reading. "Ghosts!" he scoffed. "Ted, we shall see about those so-called ghosts." I laughed and nodded.

"Spooky stories, though," I said.

"Well, I shall do my best to keep an open mind, my boy. But I shall also require a good bit of persuading before I believe the bill of goods Mason and Atkinson are peddling."

I had my doubts about the professor's attempt to keep an open mind. He was one of the most opinionated people I had ever known—though, in the end, his opinions were often borne out. Dr. Atkinson and the Reverend Mason's views about spiritual emanations would require strong evidence before the professor would be persuaded of their validity, I knew that for sure.

"Sir," I said, "are you aware of the fact that several weeks back McCauley Wilkins's wife was murdered? And that for a while he was considered the likely perpetrator? I was in Scotland at that time, but I hear it was big news in several of the daily papers."

"Papers I never deign to read. But yes, Mason did mention that fact to me. Indeed, it's the primary reason I acquiesced to his request that Wilkins be allowed to go along on our adventure. I have to admit, Ted, I haven't much taken to the fellow."

"Nor have I."

"Bankers tend to be bloodless so-and-sos," he said. "And terrible bores as well. Have you ever known a banker who wrote poetry, or who painted, or who went fishing on the weekends? A banker who was an ardent fan of Arsenal FC?"

"No, sir, I haven't. All the ones I've known have been avid Chelsea fans."

"Ha, ha. Twitting me, eh lad?"

"Actually, sir, I've never known any bankers."

"Lucky you. But Ted, I have to admit to feeling some pity for the poor fellow."

"Sir, I think you're in danger of becoming an old softie," I said with a grin.

"*Me?* An old softie? George Edward Challenger a *softie!*" he roared. "Never in your life!"

People at nearby tables looked up in alarm at the professor's outburst and waiters cast nervous looks in our direction.

One of the waiters approached us and said politely, "Will there be anything else, gentlemen?"

"Just the bill, please," I said. "Shall I arrange a conveyance for you, sir?"

"I believe I shall walk. I've been doing a lot of it this week, getting in a bit of practice for all the walking we're likely to be doing in Wales."

"Then I shall walk with you, if you don't mind."

"Excellent."

We strolled along together straight down the Strand, then skirted St. James Park on Birdcage Lane. It was a pleasant April afternoon, and as we walked along I could hear the professor humming operatic tunes most of the way. I knew he wasn't really an opera lover—and I most certainly wasn't—but his beloved Jessie had been, and the professor always humored her by going with her to the Royal Opera House. I guess he'd unconsciously absorbed some of the more famous bits.

"*Carmen*, sir?" I asked at one point.

"I believe so. Catchy tune, eh?"

I wasn't sure "tune" was the right word to describe one of Bizet's most famous arias.

8

On Friday morning the 22nd of April, the platforms at Euston Station were bustling. Lots of folks eager to get away from London for the weekend, I assumed. But we would have the first-class compartment we had booked all to ourselves. It only took the six of us a few moments to stow our bags on the racks above our heads and then to settle comfortably on the plush seats. I waited for the others to get settled, then took a seat closest to the door, just across from Professor Challenger. To his right sat Lord John Roxton and then near the window, Dr. Nathaniel Atkinson. The Reverend Charles Mason was to my left, McCauley Wilkins closest to the window on our side.

We heard the guard's whistle blow. Then the train gave a lurch before beginning its slow crawl from Euston Station. When we were well clear of the station, the train picked up steam, and as it did the wheels on the rails began to sound their familiar *clickety-clack*.

"Mac," the professor said, apparently addressing McCauley Wilkins, "I'm unclear about what has sparked your interest in ghosts. I understand the doctor's interest, and the reverend's, and even our newspaper friend's. But you strike me as an unknown country. Can you help me out?"

"If you choose to call me Mac," the man replied, sounding a bit tetchy, "then tell me what I should be calling you?"

"Professor will do. Or just Challenger." I could see the professor's grinning teeth through his thick beard.

"Professor," the Reverend Mason intervened, "McCauley's reasons are private and personal. He's here at my suggestion. He didn't really want to come on this adventure, but he agreed to do so at my request. Would you mind not poking and prodding him?"

"Well, pardon me, sir. I shall try to mind my poking and prodding."

As I studied my five companions it amused me to see how the group of us were arranged on the facing seats in the compartment. The bodies of the three men across from me sat packed chock-a-block into their row with little distance between each of them. The professor's great bulk easily took up a full third of the row, and while Lord Roxton was a trim and fit man, his broad shoulders nearly rubbed against those of Challenger and Dr. Atkinson. The doctor was a robust fellow, maybe six feet tall, and probably weighed thirteen or fourteen stone.

On my side, there was me of average height and slightly less than average weight—actually small for a former rugby outside wing; then there was the Reverend Charles Mason, a small man in every respect; and huddled by the window was McCauley Wilkins, who Mr. McArdle, my boss at the newspaper, would have described in the words of the poet as "a wee, sleekit, cowrin, tim'rous beastie." I had to smile at the thought that if a fight broke out in our compartment, one side against the other, Mason and Wilkins and I would quickly be mincemeat.

Maybe forty minutes into our journey the reverend pulled out his briar pipe and all the associated paraphernalia. He began readying it as if he were engaged in a religious ritual—scraping the bowl and knocking out the dottle, blowing through the pipe stem, carefully filling the bowl from his tobacco pouch, then tamping it down, and I don't know what-all. When he finally had it prepared to his satisfaction, he struck a match and sucked the flame down into the bowl. Victory!

Beside him, Wilkins the banker, taking his cue from his companion, lit up a fat cigar. Across from us Lord John Roxton fished in his jacket pocket and extracted a slim cheroot. "If you can't beat 'em, join 'em," he muttered.

Dr. Atkinson, with a grimace, rose to his feet and pushed open the long narrow ventilation window up above the large, fixed window. Joining forces with him, I reached out and slid that compartment door open a few inches to create a crossflow of air. The doctor nodded his appreciation. I looked across at the professor, whose eyes were shut. He seemed oblivious to the actions of the others in the compartment, though I think he was humming softly to himself.

The train chugged along steadily, passing through small towns and villages where it didn't stop. The first stop occurred two hours into our northward journey in a small village called Bletchley. Through the window I could see that a few folks disembarked and a couple of others climbed on, probably heading for Birmingham. Half an hour later we stopped again, this time in Coventry. The spire of the great cathedral soared high above the rooftops of the other buildings in the town. This was the busiest station we'd come to so far. I had never been to Coventry, but from what I could see of it through the train window, it appeared to be a very pleasant town. I suddenly remembered that there was an old phrase about sending a person to Coventry, but I couldn't recall what that was all about.

"Sir," I said looking across at the professor, what does it mean to be 'sent to Coventry'?"

"Don't worry, Ted. We would never do that to you."

"But what does it mean?"

"It means you've being ostracized."

"Yes," John Roxton agreed, "and that people ignore you or pretend you aren't even present."

"Not a compliment, then," I said.

"No, not a compliment," Lord Roxton replied.

———

At Birmingham we were scheduled to have a lengthy pause in our journey. So, when we arrived at the Birmingham Terminal Station, we all detrained so as to stretch our legs and have a sandwich in the station lunchroom. Sensing that the professor might need a small respite from Mason and Wilkins, I led him and Lord Roxton to a small table away from the others.

"You doing all right, sir?" I asked him.

"Bearing up, Ted, bearing up." Lord John smiled at his words. Roxton had said next to nothing during our entire journey thus far, but he had always been a man of few words, a man who tended to let his actions do his talking. There'd been no need for action thus far, but I suspected that might change in the future.

"These men . . . ," the professor began, but didn't finish his thought. I knew that George Challenger didn't suffer fools gladly, but he surely knew that Mason and Atkinson weren't fools. Wilkins remained an unknown quantity. Maybe he was a fool, and maybe not. Something was eating the man, that was for sure, something to do with his wife's murder, in all probability.

"Do you have any clearer read on our friend Wilkins?" I asked the professor. "He strikes me as being a tormented soul. Probably something to do with the death of his wife, don't you think?"

"I would say that either he killed her . . . or . . . "

"Or he could have prevented her from being killed but didn't," I said, finishing the professor's thought. John Roxton nodded in agreement. "Do you think it could actually be her ghost that's tormenting him?"

"What's tormenting him, Ted, comes from within him. It's a thing called guilt."

"The fellah is really rather a worm," Lord Roxton said at last, "though the others ain't so bad. The doctor seems a decent, reliable chap. The Reverend Mason, though he appears to be a true believer, is well-intentioned. I don't know how well he's likely to hold up in a pinch, though."

"And perhaps we shall see how well he and his beliefs hold up after a few days of being tested out on Ynys Enlli," Professor Challenger said.

"Oh yes, he and his beliefs are likely to be sorely tested," said Lord John.

9

McCauley Wilkins *excused himself from Dr. Atkinson and the Reverend Mason and went to use the Gents. He was finding the trip every bit as difficult as he had thought it might be. Ted Malone, the newspaper fellow, seemed all right, especially for one of that ilk. The nobleman Lord Roxton, despite his superior airs, was probably a fair-minded man. But this Professor Challenger, what a trial he was proving to be. An intellectual bully for sure. Fair-minded? Not a chance. All McCauley Wilkins could hope was that before this whole adventure was over, George Edward Challenger was going to have a rude awakening. He just hoped it wouldn't be a rude awakening that involved destructive consequences for the whole bunch of them. As for himself, McCauley Wilkins couldn't have cared less if it had destructive consequences for him. Indeed, he hoped it would.*

10

The next stage in our journey was a short one, for at Wolverhampton we were required to change trains to a more minor line that angled north to Chester. When we resumed our seats in our compartment in the first-class carriage it was in the same configuration as before, people being creatures of habit. It would take us less than two hours to reach Chester, where our rooms at the station hotel would await us. During this portion of our journey, Professor Challenger, as was his wont, dominated the conversation.

"I've been thinking about human emotions," he announced in a loud voice. "Amazing things. But I have to confess that I myself have missed out on several of the most amazing of them."

"Which ones, professor?" I asked, taking the bait.

"Most of the powerfully negative ones I'm afraid. Hate, for example. In my life I have thoroughly disliked a lot of people, but I can't say I have ever truly hated anyone. And the same goes for rage. I have sometimes experienced great anger—"

"Often, in fact," John Roxton remarked with a faint smile.

" . . . but never to the point of rage. And then there's terror. I'll admit to having been frightened a handful of times, but I've never experienced sheer terror."

"I have," I said, remembering certain experiences in the Lost World.

"What would you say is the most debilitating of the human emotions?" Dr. Atkinson asked.

"Until recently," the professor replied, "I would have said the 'green-eyed monster'."

"The greened-eyed monster of Shakespeare?" the Reverend Mason asked.

"Yes, the one who tormented poor Othello. Wouldn't you agree, Mac?" he said, directing his remark to McCauley Wilkins. "Does that square with your experience?"

"Sir," Wilkins replied after a long pause, "jealousy is certainly an extremely destructive emotion. However, I would suggest that of all the human emotions grief is the hardest to bear."

Challenger ran the fingers of his right hand through his thick beard. "You know, Mac," he said, "I think I agree with you. One never knows what a crippling emotion grief is until they've experienced it at first hand."

"And grief," the Reverend Morton said, "unlike the others, in most cases is not a short-lived thing."

"Indeed not," the professor said, "indeed not. In time it may recede somewhat, but it never goes away. It leaves a wound in the heart that never entirely heals or dissipates."

"Professor," Wilkins said, "it appears there is something the two of us can agree upon, even if it is such a trying subject as this one."

"And what about the joyous emotions?" the reverend asked, "what about them?"

"The joyous emotions?" the professor said. "Remind me what they are."

Forty-five minutes into the final stretch to Chester, the train came to a jerky halt and then sat unmoving on the tracks.

"Not again," said Dr. Atkinson. "Third time today. What can it be this time?"

A few moments later the conductor stuck his head into our compartment and said, "Sorry, sirs, they're sorting out a problem on the tracks up ahead. Shouldn't be but a few minutes 'til we'll be up and running again."

"Damme," the doctor said, "we should be up and running now."

"Well, look on the bright side," I said. "A wiser man than me once declared that 'It's better to travel hopefully than to arrive.'"

"Was that wise man named Confucius?" Charles Mason queried.

"I believe he was called Robert Louis Stevenson,"

McCauley Wilkins said.

"To be more precise," Lord Roxton said, "your Robert Louis Stevenson had borrowed that bit of wisdom from a fellah called the Buddha."

"In any case," Professor Challenger said, "it seems to me that British Rail should consider adopting the saying for their official motto."

It turned out to be more than a few minutes before we were "up and running again." But once we were, we traveled hopefully, and by early evening we had actually arrived at our destination.

11

The railroad hotel near the station in Chester was an old Victorian classic—it boasted a spacious lobby with numerous pieces of tattered furniture, a high ceiling from which hung a rarely dusted chandelier, and a wide stairway that ascended to three floors of dark hallways and gloomy rooms. I liked it.

Professor Challenger and I would be sharing a room, as would the Reverend Mason and Dr. Atkinson. McCauley Wilkins and Lord Roxton would each have their own room. I only hoped that the professor wasn't as prodigious a snorer as I feared he might be. Men of his bulk often were, though I didn't remember that as having been the case when we were in the Lost World.

After checking in, we clomped up the stairs and found our rooms. Professor Challenger immediately sprawled out on his bed and dropped instantly to sleep. While he napped I planned to poke about in this venerable old town for a bit. We would all rendezvous again at eight in the hotel dining room.

Chester, I knew, had once been a major Roman fortification, hence the city's name; it was a cathedral city also, and long stretches of the city's ancient walls were well preserved. I planned to take in what I could while it was still light out. So I made my way back down to the lobby, then stepped out in the city.

There was an entrance point to the wall walk close by, so I climbed up the few steps and began strolling. The view from atop the walls displayed the city well, and I enjoyed giving my legs a good stretch after being cooped up in the train for nearly the whole day. At one point the walls were closely adjacent to the red stone cathedral, a striking building free of the grime that clung to the sides of so many of London's great buildings. I exited from the walls to take a closer look at the cathedral's exterior.

I saw that several others were doing that as well, most of them pausing to admire the many stone carvings and gargoyles adorning the cathedral's outside walls. One of the people doing that, I realized, was McCauley Wilkins, who like me was on his own. For a long while, maybe as much as five minutes, Wilkins stood frozen before one of the stone carvings. That particular carving obviously entranced the man. Eventually he moved on, and I waited until he'd turned a corner and was out of sight before I stepped over to the spot where he had stood glued for so long.

The carving he'd been looking at sent a chill up my

spine. It was unlike nearly all the others, which depicted symbolic animals or benign carvings of people involved in normal activities. This one displayed a frightful grinning figure—surely a demon or a devil—a caped being with horns sprouting from his head and gleaming eyes. It was the kind of devilish figure often found in "Doom paintings," where demons gleefully inflict painful torments on damned souls. Wilkins had apparently been captivated by this image, and I wondered why. What was so special about it that it held his attention for so long? The image was artfully done, but I found it very creepy. Unlike Wilkins, after thirty seconds, I was happy to bid this little devil adieu and move on to the more congenial stone carvings nearby.

I wandered the streets of Chester for another half an hour, admiring the half-timbered Elizabethan buildings. This little city, I thought, was a microcosm of British history, from Roman times through the Middle Ages and the Renaissance, to the present. But despite all the evidence of its rich history, I saw no signs here of anything reminiscent of the Lost World—a world which must have once existed here, as well as everywhere else on the face of the earth during prehistoric times.

Returning to the hotel, I settled down in one of the ancient sofas just off the lobby to read the book I'd brought with me, a collection of tales by Sheridan Le Fanu. The hands on the large clock behind the registration desk registered 7:30, so I had half an hour in which to indulge myself until it was time to meet the others for our meal in the hotel dining room.

I'd finished one short and spooky little tale and was just beginning another when I realized that someone was standing only a few feet from where I was sitting. I hoped it wasn't the grinning demon I'd seen at the cathedral. I was in luck. It wasn't.

The person standing there was an attractive young woman who looked slightly apologetic for bothering me. When I had shifted my eyes from the pages of the book to her face, she spoke.

"Please pardon me for interrupting you, sir, but I couldn't help noticing what you are reading. Le Fanu is my favorite author. Are you a fan as well? He's not everyone's cup of tea."

She spoke like a cultured young woman, surely more cultured than I. She was a tallish brunette whose chestnut hair, parted in the middle, fell to her shoulders. Her oval face bore a slight smile, her gray-blue eyes were wide in anticipation of my reply.

"I'm just now acquainting myself with this author," I said. "He comes highly recommended by Mr. M.R. James, a writer whose works I do admire."

"In my humble opinion," she said with a slight lift of her shoulders, "he's even better than James." Her voice was low, soft, and pleasing.

"I bow to your superior knowledge," I said. "I'm just a

humble London newspaper hack, not a learned scholar. I'm Edward Malone, by the way, also known as Ted."

"The man who invented the Lost World? Sir, you are a writer of enviable imagination."

"I hardly invented anything," I said. "I merely reported it."

"My sisters and I drank up your every word. Of course, then we were just impressionable young children."

And now, I thought, you are an impressionable young woman. You are certainly making an impression on me. I smiled at her amiably, not sure how to proceed but not wanting the conversation to end just yet.

It did come to an abrupt end, however, when the firm voice of a man intervened. "Isabella, we are all going in now. Come along now, please."

She gave a roll of her eyes and a slight grimace flitted across her shapely lips. "Coming, Papa," she said. Then she looked at me and smiled. "It's been a pleasure meeting you, Mr. Newspaper Man. Perhaps our paths will cross again. Le Fanu. He is first rate."

I raised a hand in farewell as she trailed off behind her "Papa."

Isabella, I thought, her name is Isabella.

12

When I entered the dining room, the others were already seated around a table near the center of the room. Small groups of diners occupied several nearby tables, but the ones who seized my attention comprised a largish group off to one side and away from the general hubbub. This group was formed mostly by women, one of whom I had recently met—Isabella. The only male with them was the older man she'd called "Papa." There was a dowdy-looking older woman who I didn't think could be her mother. I wondered if a couple of the others were the sisters she'd mentioned.

I dropped into the only unoccupied chair at our table, next to McCauley Wilkins. He and I exchanged nods, but none of the others acknowledged my arrival. They were attending to Professor Challenger's impromptu oration regarding the Romans. Lord Roxton did finally glance in my direction, and for my benefit he cast a quick side-eye in the professor's direction, then shot me a grin. It took a brave man to openly scorn the professor, but Lord John was a master of subtlety and nearly always got away with it. Now and then, one of the others was bold enough to risk a comment or pose a question, but it was rare when one of them dared to express disagreement with Professor George Edward Challenger.

I only half attended to the discussion. Of greater interest to me was the group seated separately, the group that included Isabella. They were too far away for me to catch anything of their conversation, but I could tell from the rumblings of his deep voice that "Papa" was doing most of the talking.

"Mac," the professor said, pausing in his oration and addressing Wilkins, "would you be so kind as to send the rolls in my direction?"

McCauley nodded and handed the wicker basket filled with dinner rolls to the doctor, who took one and passed the basket on. I noticed that the professor took two, and I sincerely hoped the basket wouldn't be empty by the time it reached me, for I suddenly realized I was famished. I was in luck, though just barely. I snatched up the last roll, tore it in half and buttered it, just as a waiter arrived and placed a bowl of tomato and cauliflower soup down before me, the first course in the "set" dinner that we, and all the other diners, would be having. After the soup would come the roast beef and mash, and then to top things off, we would have a choice of sweets or cheese board. A half-empty carafe of red wine, claret, no doubt, sat on the table, but I drank only lemonade, wanting my senses to remain as keen as possible.

"I know that the Romans conquered and occupied Anglesey," the Reverend Mason said, "Tacitus tells us that; but did they even bother with the Llŷn Peninsula?"

"From what I've read," Dr. Atkinson said, "there's little evidence to suggest they did. Of course they weren't far away, for there was a large Roman fortress near Caernarvon. And as for Ynys Enlli, I'm quite sure they never crossed over to it."

"But the Vikings got there for sure," Challenger said. "In fact, they renamed it Bardsey Island, eschewing the Celtic name."

"Where didn't the blasted Vikings get to?" Mason moaned. "Those chaps were indefatigable."

"If they thought there was anything worth the effort to steal, and they could arrive by water," Lord Roxton said, "they didn't hesitate to help themselves. Those chaps weren't inclined to do much walking. But they did have a fondness for remote island religious sites, where the pickings were usually good and usually easy."

I tuned out the rest of the discussion and watched as the group that included Isabella prepared to leave. Her sisters, I could see, looked like lovely young girls, but they hadn't yet flowered into the beauty Isabella had achieved. The older woman with them was dressed in a plain dark gown with a high collar, her grayish hair pulled into a bun behind her head. She was gaunt and slightly stooped, her face expressionless. I feared that if she smiled her face might crack into stony shards. My guess, which later proved to be true, was that she was their governess or duenna.

As they trooped from the dining room, Isabella managed to situate herself at the rear of the procession. When she reached the doorway, she turned and glanced back in the direction of our table. She raised one hand in a gesture of farewell, a gesture I knew was intended for me. It gave me a warm feeling, and I hoped she saw my answering smile.

When they were gone, I returned my attention to our table, only to discover that Professor Challenger was looking straight at me. He stared fixedly at me for several seconds. Then I could see that his lips, buried behind his thick beard, had formed into a knowing smile. He gave me a nod, then focused his attention on his coffee cup. So far as I knew, none of the others had observed my interest in the departing group, nor had they witnessed the look the professor had just given me.

13

Drawn by some *strange compulsion, McCauley Wilkins found himself out on the moonlit streets of Chester. The time was just short of midnight. Despite himself, he knew that his feet were leading him back to the medieval cathedral. He both wanted them to and he didn't want them to. In any event, he resigned himself to the inevitable.*

It was almost as if he had unconsciously known the precise moment the waxing moon, breaking through the cloud cover, would shine down upon the crouching figure of the little demon. Now, illuminated by bright moonbeams, the stone image appeared even more malicious and malign than ever; and McCauley found that unsettling but thrilling. He'd begun to feel a strange kinship with the evil-looking little creature. It was almost as if it were his spiritual alter ego, a term he had recently heard bandied about. He felt as if this little demon were welcoming him into the brotherhood of evildoers. It was a thrilling notion, and McCauley Wilkins found himself not caring if it led to his eternal damnation. Indeed, he hoped for it.

As McCauley stared at the little demon, he imagined the creature suddenly becoming animated, its stone features becoming living flesh. As its limbs began to take on life, its lips grinned more widely, its teeth flashing in the moonlight. It detached itself from the cathedral wall and dropped down beside him, and before McCauley Wilkins realized what was happening, the demon's cold body began commingling with his into a single being. Surely it was just some strange kind of hallucination. And yet, Wilkins wasn't entirely certain of that.

14

At 9:30 in the morning we boarded the small train that would carry us around the coast of North Wales to Bangor. There was only one first-class carriage, and two of its three compartments were quickly filled by women, one of them the group that included Isabella. When we entered the compartment we had reserved, we stowed our bags on the overhead racks and assumed our customary seats.

The whistle blew, the train chugged forth. It would make several brief stops along the northern coast of Wales to pick up and discharge passengers at small towns along the edge of the Irish Sea before reaching the picturesque town of Conwy with its magnificent castle around mid-day. There we would have a longer stop. We were scheduled to reach Bangor by late afternoon. We weren't sure if we would try to find a place to spend the night there or seek out a conveyance to take us on to Caernarvon.

During the first few minutes of our train journey there

was little conversation. Even the professor seemed talked out. The reverend soon began the complex process of firing up his pipe and when he had, Dr. Atkinson, looking disgruntled, rose and opened the narrow air-vent window. The professor sat across from me his eyes closed; Lord Roxton, next to him, appeared lost in his thoughts; and McCauley Wilkins, as usual, was huddled in his corner like a wee timorous beastie.

When someone rapped firmly on our compartment door, the professor's eyes snapped open; at the same time a look of expectancy appeared on Lord John's face. The door slid partly open and a man stuck his head in. It was "Papa."

"Pardon me, gentlemen, but I was wondering if you might be willing to accommodate one more. The fact of the matter is, chattering women have driven me forth. There are limits to what a man can take, as I'm sure you can understand."

"You'd best squeeze in beside me," I said. "We've more room on this side. Reverend, mind sliding over a little closer to Mr. Wilkins?" I leaned against the compartment panel to my right and patted the spot now vacated to my left. The man smiled, breathed a sigh of relief, and plopped himself between me and the reverend Mason.

"So kind," he said. "My bag will be fine where I left it in the compartment with my daughters."

Professor Challenger gave the man a hard stare and said, "And you are, sir?"

"Baron Penhenthy," he replied. "Just now returning home from Oxford with my daughters. Isabella, my eldest, has finished the Hilary Term at Somerville College and has a short break."

Well, that puts paid to any grandiose hopes I might have had, I thought. If Isabella is a nobleman's daughter and a budding Oxford scholar, then that places her far out of reach for a bloke like me. Probably just as well, I told myself, though I couldn't help feeling somewhat dispirited.

I got to my feet and said, "Just going out to give my legs a good stretch. Back in a bit."

I left the compartment and walked the length of the little train, from the engineer's spot up front to the train's tail end behind the last of the train's three second-class carriages. It didn't take long since there were only five passenger carriages all together. As I walked past the compartment containing the baron's daughters, I saw that the older woman who'd sat with them at dinner last night seemed to be conducting some sort of drill with the younger ones. Isabella glanced up and our eyes met for a fleeting moment before I moved on. I knew that life was full of chance meetings with people of which nothing further ever came. And my encounter with Isabella was surely destined to be one of them.

In the fourteen months since Enid, my wife and Professor Challenger's only child, had died in that horrible London tram accident, I hadn't experienced even the tiniest shred of interest in any member of the opposite sex. Enid had meant everything to me. I had cherished her during our time together, and I knew that I would always cherish her memory. Now, realizing that I felt a twinge of attraction to this young woman named Isabella did not strike me as a betrayal. It was, I rationalized, a positive thing, a clear sign that I was regaining a healthy emotional equilibrium. Anyway, being a realist, I knew that Isabella, besides being far too young for me, was a nobleman's daughter while I was the commonest of commoners. Moreover, she was a budding Oxford scholar while I, though I had achieved a bit of notoriety a decade ago, was still merely a Fleet Street hack journalist. Isabella, alas, was way out of my league.

When I re-entered our compartment, no more than five minutes later, I realized the men were now in the midst of a heated discussion.

"Professor, are you defending—nay, championing—that radical heretic Pelagius? For shame, professor! For shame, I say!" The Reverend Mason's voice had reached a high pitch and he looked red in the face.

"I've no qualms about defending the so-called heretic, Mason. Many's the enlightened thinker who was labeled a heretic."

"Sir, if you subscribe to his views, it makes you a heretic as well."

"Ha, ha. Certainly wouldn't be the first time, eh, Ted." The professor glanced at me with a twinkle in his eye.

I lowered myself onto the seat beside the baron, who looked rather mystified by the heated discussion. "Afraid I'm not up on this Pelagius chap," he said softly to me.

"Nor I," I replied. I realized that Lord Roxton was looking at me, a hint of a smirk gracing his thin lips. Lord John always enjoyed it when the professor got on his high horse and charged straight into the midst of his antagonists like Achilles smiting Trojan warriors left and right beneath the towering walls of Ilium.

"Well," Dr. Atkinson said, speaking for the first time, "you have to admit that Pelagius advanced some pretty radical positions for fifth-century Christians. Challenged the notion of Original Sin, believed that sinning was a conscious choice, advocated for Free Will and rejected St. Augustine's doctrine of predestination."

"Crikey," the baron said, "must've taken a brave man to go up against St. Augustine, I should think."

"Which is what rightly led to his being branded a heretic," the reverend declared.

"Rightly?" Challenger replied. "What bosh!"

For a moment, no one spoke. "Lord John," I said into the silence, "what brought all this about?"

"'Fraid I did, Ted. Asked an innocent question about guardian angels and got more than I reckoned on."

"Surely you know, Mr. Malone," the reverend said to me, "that evil and benign spirits are in a constant struggle for our souls."

"And often times," McCauley Wilkins said, "they are indistinguishable. The good ones appear evil and evil ones appear good."

"That's where free choice comes in," Professor Challenger said. "A person must be wise enough and brave enough to distinguish between Good and Evil. Pelagius had that right."

"But what if you can't?" Wilkins said.

"Then good luck to you," the professor replied.

"It's a constant struggle," Mason said, "but one must never give up."

"There's always hope," Dr. Atkinson added.

"Until there isn't," the professor shot back, bringing to my mind our grumpy old friend Professor Summerlee in the Lost World, a man whom I missed.

"Abandon all hope, ye who enter here," I said, spouting the only line of Dante I knew.

"Well, I shall stick to Faith, Hope, and Charity, the three Christian virtues," the baron averred.

"*Fides, Spes,* and *Caritas,*" Challenger said.

"Yes, wise words to adhere to," the Reverend Mason said, nodding. At that, the conversation seemed to be over.

In any case, Professor Challenger was silent. As he glanced across at me, I thought I noticed a slight lift of his eyebrows with just a hint of a grin showing through his beard. He was a man who always enjoyed bedeviling his intellectual inferiors.

Our lunch stop in Conwy was too brief to allow us to tour the castle or walk the city walls. The baron abandoned us to check on his daughters, and we barely had time to eat before we were herded back onto the train. I was disappointed that we didn't have longer to view the attractions of the charming little town. I hoped we might on our return trip.

"Not a long trek now," the baron said, "barring the unforeseen. In an hour or so we'll pass close by my home on our way. Speaking of my home, I take it you chaps haven't as yet arranged for your evening's accommodations. Might I entice you into accepting my hospitality? We've gobs of space and it would allow us to become even better acquainted."

"How kind," Mason said. Dr. Atkinson grunted his agreement.

"I've bedded in a lot of places but never in a castle before," Professor Challenger remarked, his interest piqued.

"A castle!" blurted Wilkins.

"I would assume so," Challenger said. "Surely Baron Penhenthy's residence is the famous Penhenthy Castle."

The baron smiled. "The professor has heard of my humble abode. Yes, it is a castle—after a fashion. Mostly the work of my nineteenth-century forbears, though some more ancient bits do remain."

"Well, I for one would be delighted to stay there," Mason said. "Your offer is most kind."

"How about you, Lord Roxton?" the baron asked.

Lord John's thin lips conveyed a slight smile. "I've stayed in a good many castles," he said at last, "and all of my favorites had ghouls and ghosts."

"Then you shan't be disappointed, my dear sir," the baron said. "We've no ghouls, fortunately, but we can boast of an adequate supply of ghosts."

"*Ghosts!*" Wilkins exclaimed. "Your castle has *ghosts*?"

"Have no fear, sir. They are timid and kindly beings . . . for the most part, anyway."

15

After arriving at the station in Bangor, we hefted our bags from the racks and bid adieu to the railway. From here on we would be traveling by means of lesser conveyances, including our own two feet. Wilkins was the only one of us whose fitness concerned me. But he had a dogged perseverance about him which I hoped would serve him well.

A pair of vehicles awaited the baron's party at the station. When the young women and their copious amounts of luggage were safely loaded, they set off for home, leaving us standing behind. The baron said the drivers would return for us in about twenty minutes.

"Goodness," the Reverend Mason muttered, "I never expected to be spending the night in a castle. This is most exciting."

"A *faux* castle," Professor Challenger said. "They called them follies, and for good reason."

"Should be interesting, though," Lord Roxton said. "And we've been promised the additional attraction of ghosts."

"Don't remind me," Wilkins muttered softly.

Through a thick screen of oaks and beeches we could see the impressive outline of the top of the castle, its battlements and towers looming against a gray sky. We approached the castle by means of a causeway, spanning the remains of a man-made lake, an expanse of water no longer as broad as it once must have been, since thick clusters of rushes now impinged upon its edges. I could make out a few swans gliding gracefully through them. It was an elegant scene, right out of the pages of *Ivanhoe* or "The Lady of Shallot"—"*And sometimes thro' the mirror blue / The knights come riding two and two . . . ,*" I mused to myself.

The narrow roadway entered the castle's great gateway and passed beneath an impressive portcullis. We then found ourselves in a cobbled quadrangle courtyard surrounded by the castle's great wings. Before us loomed an archway which I assumed was the main entrance to the modernized domestic portion of the castle. The steep steps that led to its massive doorway were flanked by great stone flower pots which appeared to hold recent plantings that I, a city lad, couldn't identify.

The baron greeted us and we all trooped into the entrance hall behind him. Along the walls on both sides armored figures stood guard, and gracing the gray stone walls above them coats of arms and clusters of medieval weapons were artfully displayed. My companions, perhaps aside from Professor Challenger, seemed appropriately impressed. It all struck me, with my plebian tastes, as being a bit excessive, but I wasn't ungrateful for the baron's hospitality.

"Well, then, let's get you chaps settled," he said. "Then we can give some thought to our evening's repast."

A member of his domestic staff led us up a broad stairway to a long gallery off of which were a series of guest bedrooms, one for each of us. "The castle has seventy rooms," our guide said, "not all of which are regularly maintained, but I think you will find that your rooms for the night will prove quite satisfactory."

Professor Challenger was placed in the first of the rooms and I in the sixth and last, which was slightly smaller than the others. I dropped my bag beside the foot of the bed then stepped over to the window, which afforded a splendid view out over the lake and the deer park beyond. Behind thin clouds the sun was just now dipping low in the west. Off in that direction, not too far away, lay the Llŷn Peninsula and just beyond it our goal, the tiny island called Ynys Enlli.

An hour later we were summoned to the dining room where the ladies awaited us. The baron's wife, Lady Penhenthy, was a gracious dark-haired woman, tall and elegant and sedately attired in a mauve gown. She sat at one end of the long table, the baron at the other, their four daughters—Isabella, Carmelita, Josella, and Rosalinda—all sat in a row down one side, with our party sitting on the other. I had been placed closest to

Lady Penhenthy, across from the youngest daughter, whose name I now knew was Rosalinda. The old nanny or tutoress or whatever she was—she was never introduced—was seated smack in the center of the row with the baron's daughters. Isabella sat at the far end, to her father's left, right across from Professor Challenger. At one point our eyes met, but placed where we were, we had no opportunities to speak.

It was a pleasant meal, the conversation subdued, the young women—with the exception of Rosalinda—shy in the presence of strangers. Professor Challenger was on his best behavior, exchanging small talk with the baron. At one point, when there was a lull in conversation, he asked Isabella what subject currently excited the young women of Somerville College. She thought about it a moment before saying, "I suppose it's the writings of Carl Jung, the Swiss psychologist who is something of a protégé of Sigmund Freud. Have you read him?"

"Just a bit, though I am no expert on him. I believe 'introversion' and 'extroversion' are terms of his coinage. And of course the collective unconscious."

"Ah, the collective unconscious," Dr. Atkinson said, "fascinating concept."

"What does that mean, the collective unconscious?" asked the baron.

"I shall defer to your daughter," Atkinson said.

"Well," Isabella began, "in simplest terms, it's the notion that preserved in our subconscious minds are important cultural common denominators that have come down to us after passing though many successive generations. These are common denominators that we share both with our forebears and with each other."

"Like what?" Professor Challenger asked. "Taboos? Deep-seated notions of morality?"

"Yes. Deeply rooted attitudes, biases, fears—for a simple example, take the fear of spiders and snakes, which is innate to most people. More importantly, psychological predilections."

"Do all of us sitting around this table share these things?" Dr. Atkinson asked.

"Yes, at least to some degree. That's the suggestion, at any rate."

"Fear of ghosts?" I said, half facetiously. My remark brought a laugh from Rosalinda, across from me, but only smiles from the others. I would have liked to have a sight of Wilkins's face, but from where I was sitting I couldn't.

After the Carl Jung conversation died out, Lady Penhenthy said to me, "I understand that all of you are making a pilgrimage together. We do get the odd pilgrim passing through from time to time, but I don't recall seeing anything like the six of you before. Are you particularly devout?"

"A few of us are. In my case," I said, "it's more a matter of curiosity. I'd heard rumors of the holy island and thought I should experience it for myself." I didn't admit that I was on assignment for my newspaper.

"I am not Welsh," Lady Penhenthy said; "my own heritage is Spanish, but I've come to appreciate the rich culture of Wales and their love of the old legends and myths. I found Lady Guest's translation of *The Mabinogion* quite extraordinary. If you haven't read it, you certainly should. The girls have been steeped in Welsh lore since childhood. Welsh music, too. Rosie," she said, nodding toward Rosalinda sitting to her right, "is an accomplished flutist and is well on her way to becoming a fine harpist. The tapestries, by the way," she said, waving a hand in the direction of the wall behind her, "reflect some of the old Celtic legends."

"Papa," Rosie called down to the other end of the table, "after our meal, might we be allowed to take our guests on a tour of the keep?"

"You must ask them, Rosie. They may be too tired after their journey."

"Do you think we will find it to our liking?" I asked Rosalinda.

"Oh, sir," she said, grinning, "if it doesn't give you the creeps, nothing will."

"Rosie, don't be trying to frighten our guests," the Lady admonished.

"If you promise it will give me the creeps, I shall certainly come," I said.

"I promise," she said, crossing her heart.

The castle's keep, its high central tower, although greatly restored in the nineteenth century, preserved more of the original medieval structure than any other part of the castle.

The girls, Rosie in the lead, led us up the winding stone steps all the way to the flat, unroofed portion at the top. There in the twilight we could lean on the guard rails and look out over the broad expanse of surrounding forest. "In the daylight," Isabella said, "you can see all the way to the Menai Straits and Anglesey beyond. It's too dark now."

"Ah, Anglesey," Professor Challenger said, "the Druids' Isle."

"If I'm remembering my Tacitus correctly," the Reverend Mason said, "the Romans did a good job of putting paid to the Druids."

"And yet," Lord Roxton observed dryly, "the Celts are still here, are they not, and the Romans are long gone."

"Come!" Rosie sang out gleefully, "now, we must all go down to the dungeons! They're the best part." I noticed Wilkins shudder.

Wilkins and I waited until the others had begun clambering down ahead of us. The dark stair steps were only illuminated at intervals by dim lights, so I proceeded cautiously. I realized that Wilkins lagged behind me, the dungeons apparently holding little attraction for him. Soon the sound of the others' footsteps receded into the distance below, and I could hear Wilkins bumbling along slowly on the steps above me. As I proceeded downward, I carefully navigated the twists and turns in the ancient stairway.

16

McCauley Wilkins remained *alone atop the keep's roof for a full minute after the others had begun descending the narrow stone stair steps to the tower's lowest level. Then slowly, reluctantly, he began groping his way downward. He proceeded cautiously, for the passage was poorly lit and there were unexpected twists and turns. Now the others were gone and he was alone. He wasn't happy to be there. The place gave him the creeps.*

Wilkins hadn't found the castle as charming as the others had, and this keep especially unnerved him. He was proceeding slowly, keeping his eyes on the steps immediately ahead of him, when he heard an unexpected noise coming from below, a kind of moaning sound. Suddenly through an opening in the stonework below him for a brief moment he saw a face. The light was dim and he didn't have a clear view of the section he was about to reach. He took a few more cautious steps. Suddenly, a head materialized in the opening. It bore a crazed and demonic look, like the head of the figure he'd seen at Chester Cathedral. It was horned and red-eyed and its open mouth displayed sharp, bestial teeth. It looked like it could be the Devil's own spawn. Wilkins's terror was so great he could hardly breathe.

Then from the creature's mouth came a low, raspy voice: "Wil-kins! Wil-kins. At last you've come!"

McCauley Wilkins remained frozen in his tracks, his face transfixed by fear: his nostrils flared, his eyes bulged, his jaws gaped.

For a long minute he stood there as if paralyzed. Then, slowly, the sight before him began to dissolve. It began reforming into something different, something far more benign. And after a couple more seconds Wilkins realized that he knew to whom this face and creepy voice belonged.

"Ted Malone!" he bellowed, "you stinking rotter! What do you think you're playing at?"

"Malone?" Ted replied. "Oh no, sir, I am not Ted Malone, I am the Ghost of Penhenthy Castle."

"Ha, ha. Very funny, Ted—you sadistic bastard. After I kill you, then maybe you can become one of the castle's ghosts."

Ted Malone reached out and gripped Wilkins's arm. "Gave you a bit of a fright, eh, McCauley?" he said with a chuckle. "Sorry if I scared you. Didn't really mean to, you know. Just having a bit of fun."

"Didn't really mean to! Hah! That was no bit of fun! That was a mean and vicious thing to do. Might need to revise my opinion of you, Ted."

"Mea culpa. I'm really sorry, McCauley. I hope you won't bear a grudge."

"Well . . . I shall have to think about that."

Wilkins joined Malone, and then the two of them proceeded downward together without speaking. It took them a couple of minutes to locate the others clustered inside a cell at the very bottom of the keep, a relief to McCauley Wilkins.

17

When Wilkins and I reached the cramped and ill-smelling cell at the very bottom of the keep, there stood the girls and our other companions. They were staring at Professor Challenger, my father-in-law, who stood knee-deep in a pile of moldy straw. His wrists wore shackles and the manacles on his feet were attached to chains connected to a great iron ring bolted to one of the walls.

"For the next week," Rosie proclaimed, "this vicious criminal shall be fed on nothing but bread and water. That will teach him to steal eggs from the vicar's hen house."

"I did no such thing," Challenger bleated. "I am an innocent man."

"Hah. We caught you red-handed. How else could you explain the yellow egg yolk that was all over the front of your tunic, eh? How would you explain that?"

"I can't help it if I am sometimes a careless eater. I just am.

Ted Malone can affirm the truth of that, right, Ted?"

"I can," I said. "It's definitely true. Professor Edward Challenger is the sloppiest eater I have ever known. I don't think I have ever seen him of a morning without splotches of egg yolk all down the front of his tunic."

"Well, all right, then," Rose said, "it seems we must let him go *this* time." Then she stepped over to the professor and produced a large and ornate but rusty key. She began unlocking the manacles. "In future, though, we shall be keeping a close eye on this wily rapscallion."

"I certainly would if I were you," I said. Challenger gave me the bent-eye. He'd apparently grown tired of this little joke at his expense. The manacles off, he rubbed his wrists to get some feeling back into them. He still looked a bit tetchy.

Since we were all ready to call it a night, we declined the baron's offer of a final glass of port. I had hoped for an opportunity to have a private audience with Isabella, but that never eventuated, for all the ladies disappeared before we trooped up the stairs to where our rooms awaited us. When we exchanged our goodnights, the professor still sounded grumpy and Wilkins still looked jittery.

In my room the counterpane had been turned down and a light glowed dimly on the bed stand. There was no heat and the chilly room was mostly enveloped in shadows. I slipped into my flannel nightshirt and crawled into bed. I wasn't in a reading mood—besides, the light was too poor—so I lay there staring toward the window that looked out over the lake. The castle was now shrouded in silence, and I could just make out night noises coming from the forest. I thought I heard splashing sounds from the lake, and somewhere off in the woods an owl hooted. Then there came the high-pitched bark of a fox. I shuddered. An owl and a fox, two of Nature's most cunning predators.

As I lay there, I suddenly had a strong feeling that I was not alone. Someone—or some *thing*—was in the room with me. I could feel their eyes upon me. Then from the far corner of the room I heard a small rustling sound. Was my imagination playing tricks on me? Or was I experiencing a visitation from one of the ghosts of Penhenthy Castle? For the briefest moment I thought I caught a glimmer of luminous eyes from down near the foot of the bed. It was there and then it was gone. C'mon, Ted Malone, I told myself, you're a tough London street kid. What is there to be afraid of? Besides, the baron had assured us that the ghosts in this castle were benign creatures. I hoped to heaven that was true.

I pulled the counterpane over my head and snuggled down into my bed. Jittery as I was, sleep didn't come quickly. It took the better part of an hour, but eventually blessed sleep did find me.

The first thing I heard in the morning was a childish voice calling, "Graymalkin! Where are you? Graymalkin, you naughty girl! Where have you gone?"

I poked my head out from beneath the covers. There before me I saw a pair of bright green eyes staring at me from the foot of my bed. They were the eyes of a cat. No doubt they were the eyes of Graymalkin.

"Rosie," I called out, "she's in here. You can come into the room."

"Oh, there you are, you little rascal," Rosie said, rushing into the room. "I hope you haven't disturbed the nice man."

"I'm grateful to her, Rosie. She kept my feet warm all night long." I didn't mention that she had also contributed a good bit to my anxiety concerning ghosts.

"This cat is the very devil," Rosie said. "I hope she didn't place an evil spell on you."

"Is Graymalkin given to doing that?"

"This cat is not actually a *cat*," Rosie said. "She's a witch."

"Some witches are good witches," I said.

"Maybe so, but not *this* one. It will be a week or two before you find out if she's placed a spell on you. Oh, and I was supposed to tell you that breakfast is available in the kitchen dining area whenever you want it. Some of your friends have already gone down.

"Come on, Graymalkin," she said, scooping up the cat. "We've bothered the gentleman long enough."

18

I was the last one down for breakfast. I could see that the others were nearly finished, but rashers of bacon and a sufficiency of scrambled eggs still remained in the chafing dish for me to fill my plate. Lord Roxton gave me a welcoming nod, but the others didn't even look up. Wilkins, it seemed to me, made a special effort to avoid my eye. I was relieved to see no egg-yolk stains on the front of the professor's gray jumper, though it looked like he'd managed to drag the cuff of one sleeve through a spill of tea near his plate. Soon I was the only one remaining as the others returned to their rooms to gather up their gear.

But, in fact, I *wasn't* the only one still in the breakfast room. Isabella was there too. Sitting off by the windows that looked out on the castle gardens, she was wrapped in an emerald shawl, her face bearing a wistful, faraway look. It was like a lovely pre-Raphaelite painting by Holman Hunt or William Morris of a young woman with a roses-and-cream complexion. Her face was framed by a tumble of chestnut curls. I was tempted to call out a greeting to her, but I chose not to, thinking it rude to interrupt her reverie. So I sat there and admired her in silence as I ate a few bites of breakfast.

When I got up to leave, Isabella was still lost in her brown study. And so, to my disappointment, we exchanged no parting words.

The baron had graciously arranged for our transport to Caernarvon in one of his large vehicles. He, Lady Penhenthy, and Rosie stood on the steps beside the courtyard to bid us farewell, Rosie holding Graymalkin cradled in her arms. As he went by, Professor Challenger said, "Hello, Puss." He reached out and patted the cat's head. "You have a fine-looking cat," he said to Rosie.

"She's not a cat," Rosie shot back. "She's a witch."

"Oh, my," said Challenger, opening his eyes wide, his grinning teeth showing through his thick beard.

Not wanting the visit to end on a rude note, Lady Penhenthy said, "I hope you will stay another night with us on your return. You would be most welcome."

"Yes, please do," the baron added. "We shall look for you in about six or seven days, eh?"

"Most kind of you," Challenger said, "most kind indeed."

"Yes, do come back," Rosie added. "I will want to know if the witch's spell really worked on Mr. Malone." She gave me a wicked grin. I gave her a tight-lipped smile and shot my eyes back and forth, pretending to be nervous.

As we climbed into the conveyance, I said to Wilkins, "That cat really is a witch, you know. Rosie is quite certain the cat has put a spell on me and it might well be true." McCauley gave me a squinty-eyed stare.

19

Hard rain poured down on the cobbled streets of the small gray town of Caernarvon tucked between the high peaks of Snowdonia and the Menai Straits. The six of us, though, were snug and dry inside the cozy public house-cum-inn only a stone's throw from the great Edwardian castle. We could just see its imposing outline through the heavy veil of slanting rain.

When we'd reached the little town we had several bits of luck. The inn—which, predictably, was called The Prince of Wales—had more than enough available rooms to accommodate all of us; and just as fortunately, when we told the publican where we were headed, he said he knew a local farmer who planned to transport a lorry-load of sheep's wool first thing in the morning to the woolen mill in Pwllheli. For a small fee, the fellow would surely be happy to let us ride along in the back of his vehicle. The innkeeper, a veritable fount of information, also proclaimed that the weather for the next several days would be dry and sunny. That was welcome news, because if we had to hoof it the twenty or so miles from Pwllheli to Aberdaron at the far end of the Llŷn Peninsula, at least we wouldn't have to do it in inclement weather. That was our hope, anyway, though we knew that Welsh weather can be notoriously fickle.

We settled into the inn's dining area for our midday repast, the innkeeper happy to have our business. Before long he placed before us bowls of potato and leek soup, a basket of freshly baked bread, a platter loaded with slices of cheese, pickled onions, and a bowl of piccalilli. He said that steak-and-kidney pudding was on its way.

When Professor Challenger bit halfway through a pickled onion, onion juice squirted down into his thick matted beard. He grinned at me. "Pickled onions, Ted, best medicine I know of for preventing colds. Here, have one."

"Maybe later, thanks, if I still have room after the steak-and-kidney pudding."

"Well, at least have a jar of this Double Dragon ale, eh? Glorious stuff. I think this no-alcohol regimen you've set for yourself, my lad, is sheer nonsense."

"Quite likely. But since I've already made a good start on it, I think I'll stick with it for now." I didn't know myself why I'd suddenly become so abstemious. Maybe subconsciously I knew that being on a pilgrimage, as we ostensibly were, required a degree of self-abnegation.

"Perhaps your shadow has taken charge of you, Ted," Lord Roxton said, half-seriously.

"His *shadow?*" blurted Wilkins.

"Sounds like we're about to hear more Jungian stuff and nonsense," Professor Challenger said.

"No, it's not nonsense," Dr. Atkinson asserted, in support of Roxton. "That young woman last night didn't bring up Jung's notion of the shadow, but I've always found that to be one of his more persuasive suggestions."

"Is the shadow kind of like Freud's id?" the Reverend Mason asked.

"No, not really, though that comparison readily springs to mind. It's not just about sex, like Freud's id."

"More like Dr. Jekyll and Mr. Hyde?" I proffered.

"Dr. Atkinson, set these chaps straight, eh?" Lord John said.

"Not surprising that you would think of the id, Mason, or you of Stevenson's tale, Ted," Atkinson said. "They have some things in common with Jung's notion of one's shadow. But as I understand it, the shadow isn't so exclusively associated with our more animalistic impulses. For Jung, the shadow is actually part of the ego, not the id. It represents all those things the ego tries to suppress or deny, things we aren't consciously aware of but that are still a very real part of us. Freud's id is associated only with our more primitive urges—fear, hunger, sexual desires—urges that beg for immediate gratification. Jung's shadow does have negative aspects but it also has quite positive ones. Among other things, it's connected to our creativity. In the shadow the negative urges and behaviors are suppressed beneath our level of consciousness with good intentions. Sometimes—take, for example, our friend Ted—his puckish sense of humor surfaces to override his normally sensible demeanor. Sometimes in highly creative people their shadow only emerges or is manifested in their art—take, for example, T. S. Eliot or G. B. Shaw, normally quiet, socially responsible people. But in some others, people like Oscar Wilde or Pablo Picasso, their shadow comes to dominate their entire being. And then there is a third group of folks, folks like Professor Challenger here, who—"

"Sounds like a load of rubbish to me," bellowed Professor Challenger, breaking into the doctor's disquisition. "Don't you think so too, Wilkins?" Like me, the professor had noticed the London banker's growing agitation.

"To be honest," Wilkins said, "I would have no objection to changing the subject. I've heard enough about this Jung chap to last me a good long while. In fact, I think I shall be spending some time alone in my room this afternoon." He got to his feet, waved a general goodbye, and headed for the stairs.

20

I sat by the mullioned windows in the snug where there was sufficient light for me to read, a glass of lemonade on the table beside me. My companions were gathered round a table just a few feet away playing whist. They'd had a spirited argument over whether they should play cribbage or whist, and whist won out when the doctor and the reverend insisted they would *not* play cribbage, a game they considered low-class. That struck me as ironic, since Lord Roxton, the person of highest social status amongst us, was the one who'd suggested cribbage.

While the others played cards, I took a moment to scratch out a quick letter to Mr. McArdle, my editor at *The News Gazette*, to update him and let him know he probably wouldn't be hearing from me again until after we'd concluded our little adventure out on Ynys Enlli—whatever that adventure turned out to be. I knew that despite his outward show of indifference, he was a warm-hearted man who cared a lot about me and my well-being.

After I finished dashing off my letter, I paused to reflect a moment on what all of us thought we were doing, what our intentions were. I knew that our goal was the small islet of Ynys Enlli, believed to be a holy refuge, a place to which countless pilgrims since the Middle Ages had journeyed. I knew that it was a venerated Christian site, but that like many of them scattered throughout Europe, it had also been a holy site long before the advent of Christianity. Ynys Enlli was a place that had been sacred to the ancient Celts. They believed it to be a place where at certain times of the year the boundary between the physical world and the spirit world became blurred; and that at such times it might even become possible for beings from one realm to pass into the other realm, humans into the Celtic Otherworld, otherworldly beings into the human realm.

We had set off from London's Euston Station on Friday, April 22nd. It was now Sunday the 24th, and I knew we should reach Aberdaron in two more days, the 26th. Then, if the weather cooperated, we'd make the short crossing to the island on Wednesday the 27th. That was cutting it close, but if all went well, we should have at least a couple of days on the island before the Eve of Beltane, April 30th. That was our hope.

Exactly what we hoped or expected to experience there was unclear to me. It was probably something different for each one of us. Professor Challenger, with his antipathy to spiritualism, was probably hoping nothing out of the ordinary would occur and he could debunk the whole business. For Dr. Atkinson and Lord Roxton, I think they were both entering into the thing with an open mind, hoping to discover some new truths about psychic phenomena. McCauley Wilkins, aided by the Reverend Mason, had come in hopes of resolving some personal crisis, perhaps a crisis involving the death of his wife. As for me, I was just along for the ride. My hope was to get an interesting story out of it for the newspaper. An added bonus for me was having crossed paths with Isabella, although she had turned out to be the daughter of a nobleman.

My thoughts then swerved from Ynys Enlli to Isabella, a fascinating young woman whose behavior thus far struck me as somewhat enigmatic. Her demeanor toward me had initially been warm and friendly; but then at the baron's castle, she'd acted indifferent and aloof. This morning when I'd come down to breakfast she'd totally ignored me. It was as if she was lost in her own world. Isabella certainly appeared to be a young woman of independent spirit, something I quite admire in a woman. And she possessed the two other things I most admire in a woman: intelligence and beauty. I was grateful to her for re-awakening in me feelings and desires I hadn't had since the death of my wife, Enid. For many months now I had been emotionally numb. I hadn't really been living, just going through the motions. It was good to begin to feel alive once again.

Enid, my deceased wife and Professor Challenger's only child, a woman I'd loved and cherished, had possessed all three of those attributes—beauty, intelligence, and an independent spirit. I much admired the fact that she had chosen to defy social convention by taking a menial position in the office of *The News Gazette*, a London newspaper of somewhat dubious reputation and the paper for which I myself worked. That was where Enid and I first came to know each other. It was after several months of our working together that we simultaneously discovered that we were falling in love. But her tragic death had opened a deep chasm in my life, one I didn't think would ever be filled. I missed her greatly. But at the same time, I had no illusions that I would be encountering her spirit when we reached Ynys Enlli. On that score I sided with my father-in-law, who scoffed at such a likelihood.

I had picked up my book and was about to start in on another of the short stories when I heard the sound of humming coming from the card table. Being familiar with that habit of his, I knew the person humming could only be Professor Challenger.

"Professor," said the Reverend Mason, "is that you humming 'Twinkle, Twinkle Little Star'?"

"Indeed I am not, sir. The mellifluent tune engaging your ears, which I confess is mine, is not 'Twinkle, Twinkle Little Star.' It is 'Baa Baa Black Sheep.'"

"Thinking about our ride tomorrow in the lorry with the farmer's load of sheep's wool?" Dr. Atkinson asked.

"Sometimes tunes just come upon me," the professor said, "sent, no doubt, by my shadow. But the thing that's always struck me as odd about that particular nursery rhyme is that the primary speaking voice is that of a sheep, a black sheep at that, one who is able to dispose of his three bags of wool as he chooses—one to his master, one to his dame, and one to some little boy who lives or cries or whatever, in the lane."

"Spoken by a sheep," I said, from my seat in the snug, "makes me think of the speaking voice in the Twenty-third Psalm, which is also that of a sheep."

"Sir," said the reverend glaring at me, "your remark borders on blasphemy. I urge you to be mindful that when speaking of the Scriptures, one must speak respectfully."

"I meant no disrespect, Reverend. But surely you aren't telling me that voice in the famous psalm *isn't* that of a sheep?"

"Only metaphorically, sir, only metaphorically. If you weren't just an ignorant newspaper man, you would know that that is often the case in King David's poetry."

I was stung by the man's insult. But I managed to bite my tongue and hold back the rude reply that *this* ignorant newspaperman was tempted to make. I saw my father-in-law give me a small nod of approval for my restraint.

For a moment no one else chose to say anything. I certainly hadn't meant to rile the man. I was simply making what I thought was a pertinent observation.

Then Professor Challenger said, staring the reverend in the eye, "I've always wondered if "Mary Had A Little Lamb" was about the Virgin Mary and the Lamb of God. What's your opinion on that, Reverend Mason?" But the reverend didn't take the bait.

Again there was silence until Lord Roxton finally said, "You know, professor, I too thought the tune you were humming sounded a lot like 'Twinkle, Twinkle Little Star.'"

"Same tune, different nursery rhymes," Challenger said. Then, he snatched up the deck of cards and shuffled them noisily. He dealt the cards and the men resumed their game. I picked up my book, found my place, and began reading about ghosts.

21

From the small window *in his tiny second floor room, McCauley Wilkins stared out toward the huge castle. The rain had finally slackened and now the tall hexagonal towers could be seen soaring skyward like staunch gray sentinels against the slate-colored firmament. They had stood there like that for more than 600 years, since Edward I had overseen the construction of his most impressive castle late in the thirteenth century—the castle where Edward II, the original Prince of Wales, had been born. Like everything else, the great towers of Caernarvon Castle would eventually crumble and fall. But not any time soon, McCauley told himself. It was something he would never have to worry about.*

Behind him McCauley heard a floorboard creak. He swung about but the room was empty. Suddenly his eye was drawn to the small wall mirror just to the left of his bed. And then he gasped. There, in the mirror's reflection, he saw a woman standing at the foot of his narrow bed, no more than five feet away. She had a half-smile on her full lips; a gleam of light shone from her deep brown eyes that were framed by long, dark lashes. She was a beautiful woman and one whom McCauley had loved. Still looking at the image in the mirror, he ran his eyes over her white blouse, decorated across the front with large red flowers. But as he looked closer, he realized they weren't flowers. He stared at her in astonishment. Finally he whispered, "Felicity, I didn't do it."

Her smile broadened. "I know, love," she said. "But you as good as did it."

"No," came his whispered reply, "no . . . no."

"Oh yes," she said, her head dipping forward twice to emphasize her words.

McCauley whirled about and reached towards her. His hand touched nothing but empty air. Felicity was gone. Had she even been there? Was she just an illusion, another of his strange hallucinations?

Then he realized that a familiar fragrance—it was the fragrance of Yardley's English Roses—still lingered in the room. McCauley Wilkins slumped down onto the bed, his head cradled by his hands. He couldn't prevent himself from weeping.

22

McCauley Wilkins and the Reverend Mason, the two smallest men in our party of six, squeezed in with Evan Jenkins, the sheep farmer who was giving us a lift to the Llŷn Peninsula. The rest of us clambered into the back of the lorry, along with our baggage, and sprawled out atop the bags filled with wool. The morning sun had yet to appear above the tops of the high mountains to our left, and I was glad I'd thought to bring along a warm jumper. The others were similarly attired.

Mr. Jenkins said he was a devout man himself, and though he'd never been to Ynys Enlli, he approved of our endeavor. "We can make a quick stop, if yor a-wantin', at Saint Beuno's Church, no trouble a-tall. Most pilgrims make that their first stop on the peninsula. It's the only church that's on our route ta the woolen mill today, so's the rest o' 'em you'll hafta do by yor ownselves as ya hike out ta the tip end of the peninsula."

"That's grand," the reverend replied. "Your assistance

and advice is much appreciated."

We trundled along at a slow pace, and despite the terrible condition of the unmetalled roadway, those of us in the back rode in relative comfort cushioned by the bags of wool. Less than an hour later the farmer pulled off at the church he'd mentioned. He said he could afford us half an hour to check the place out. I noticed that on the surrounding wall there was a plaque that indicated we were indeed on the pilgrims' route.

I've always liked ancient churches, and inside this one were several very old woodcarvings that I found quite interesting. Architecturally the building itself wasn't remarkable, but standing near the southwestern wall was an ancient upright stone sundial.

"Know what that is?" the professor asked, after he'd materialized next to me.

"Looks rather like a sundial," I replied.

"You are nearly correct, but it's not in fact a sundial. Inspect it closely. You'll see that those division marks don't represent hours."

"What do they represent?"

"This thing is actually called a tide dial, a close cousin to the usual sundial. The markings represent the different tides, not the hours of the day."

"Tides? That makes no sense."

"A tide in this case means a time of worship. Nothing to do with ocean tides. The monks' day was divided into eight periods of worship. This dial tells them which one is next and when it begins."

"Not much good for that at night, I should think."

"No, the monks tended to spend much of their time at night alone in solitary prayer and contemplation. You might have made a good monk yourself, Ted," he said with a smile.

I couldn't help laughing at that. "I can't picture myself as a monk, sir."

"On this pilgrimage of ours some of your monkish tendencies have already surfaced."

"Hah. Well, then, I'd better begin nipping them in the bud."

"Monks had to make vows of poverty, chastity and obedience. As I say, Ted, I think you're well on your way."

"I want nothing to do with any of the three, sir. Though when it comes to poverty, I may not have much choice."

It was almost noon when the farmer dropped us off on the high street in Pwllheli. We paid him and offered to buy him lunch, but he declined. He just wanted to get his wool to the mill, collect his fee, and head back to his farm. "Good luck on your journey," he said. "Offer up a prayer or two for me and my sheeps, if ya'd be so kind." Then he was away.

With several hours of daylight still remaining, we considered setting off on foot for Aberdaron. But the dark billowing clouds to the west dissuaded us. Anyway, we could probably make it a one-day trek if we got off to an early start in the morning.

The town boasted only one hotel, and it wasn't the Ritz. "Any port in a storm," Dr. Atkinson said. And it was an hour later that the actual storm broke. We'd been wise not to push on. When a break in the rain finally came, we wandered out and explored the shops for provisions. "Not likely to be much in Aberdaron, and little or nothing out on the island itself, so we'd best get it while we can," the professor said. Knowing that tomorrow would be an arduous day, we napped and read and planned to have an early night after our evening meal.

The hotel's bar, lounge, and dining room were one large, dark and dingy, wood-paneled, low-beamed affair. Our meal of lamb chops and mash, however, was a truly delightful repast. "Just enough time for a post-prandial drink," said Dr. Atkinson, "then it's off to bed."

A few locals had wandered in by that point, including a trio of early middle-aged women. They looked us over with interest, and the Reverend Mason, being an outgoing chap, engaged them in conversation. As they were chatting amiably, a large group of rough-looking men came tumbling in. They glanced toward Mason, who was talking to the women, and then stared fixedly at the rest of us. McCauley Wilkins, appearing nervous at the look of these fellows, slipped away quietly. That worked for our "wee, sleekit, timorous beastie," but it didn't work for the rest of us.

One of the men walked up to the bar and intentionally

jostled against Dr. Atkinson, causing him to spill his drink. "So, Dai Williams," the fellow said loudly to the barman so everyone else in the room could hear, "you ain't so particular about who ya serve in here, eh?"

"No need to cause trouble, Rob. These chaps have been real gents."

"Ya like the color o' their money, doncha, Dai. Guess ya don't mind the stink of Englishmen if they be well-heeled enough for ya."

The professor nudged me. "Welsh nationalists, I'm thinking," he whispered. "This might get nasty."

"Rob," said one of the women, "don't ya be makin' no scene, mind ya?"

"Don't you be tellin' me what to do or not do, Ceri. You ain't me mum."

"I think we should be helpin' Dai out and riddin' this place of English scum," another man said. "Chase these wankers outta here with their tails between their legs." The others laughed, and one of them said, "I'm with ya, Hywel." The group of men crowded forward, pinning us back against the bar. There was a dozen of them, just five of us, and one of our five, despite being reasonably fit, was well along in years. These Welshmen all looked to be in their twenties or thirties, rough, tough, laboring men.

One of the men approached me and stared into my face intently. "Say," he said after a long moment's study, a surprised look on his face. "Don't I be knowin' you? Would you not be Ted Malone, the flying outside half for the Fulham Aces?"

Wow, I thought, who is this bloke? And how in the world does he know me? Then it came to me. "Davie Jones?" I asked. "Is that you, mate? Why, you look just as fit as you did ten years ago."

He grinned, reached out, and gave my shoulder a squeeze. "You was a real flyer, Malone. Maneuvered yor skinny arse right by me for a try. Just the once, mind you. After that I got ya good."

"You certainly did, Davie. You were one hell of a tackler. My ribs still haven't fully recovered. Man, you were one hard hitter." Davie laughed.

Then he turned to his compatriots, a big smile on his face. "This here fella was a hell of a rugby player. He played so good ya mighta thought he were a Welshman and not just some feckless Irishman a-playin' for a bunch o' English pansies. Fellas, this here is Ted Malone, the Fulham Flier."

I waved hello to the others who murmured various greetings.

"What's bringin' ya to our fair homeland, Ted?"

"Believe it or not, Davie, we're pilgrims, heading for Ynys Enlli."

"They're pilgrims, lads. Doesn't that help to forgive 'em for being Englishmen?"

The mutterings and groans from the others seemed to me to create some uncertainty about that. "No, not entirely," I heard one voice say.

"Davie," I said, "is this your local rugby club?"

"Nah. But one or two o' 'em has played a good bit o' rugger. Nah, Ted, this here is our local all-male choir. Just finished our weekly practice where we worked up a goodly thirst."

"Gosh, Davie, your all-male choir. I'll bet you guys are great."

"Not half-bad, if I say so myself. Going to participate in the Eisteddfod this year. Maybe win a prize."

"D'ya think the fellas would be willing to sing something for us?"

"What about it, fellas, you willing to sing for our visitors?"

None of them objected, so Davie said, "Anything special ya might be wantin' ta hear?"

"Do you think you could sing 'Lywyn Onn'?" the professor said, speaking to them for the first time. It surprised me that Challenger knew the Welsh title for "The Ash Grove"—but then one should never be surprised at what the professor knows.

"Ah, you must be a sentimental fellow, my friend. Yes, I believe we could. How's about it, chums?"

"Let's do it," one of them yelled out. And in the next moment they launched into it. As they sang the lovely traditional Welsh song, I heard the professor humming along with them.

We, and the handful of others in the room, applauded

loudly when they'd finished.

"Splendid," said the professor, "just splendid." My father-in-law looked a little teary-eyed and Davie reached out and patted his shoulder.

"Say, old fella, I couldn't help hearin' you humming along with us. Makes me think you must be a musical cove also. We've sung one for you, so how about you singing one for us?" I had to admit, up to that point in my life I had never even once heard the professor sing, nothing more than hum.

"Well, yes, I like to think I'm a musical fellow, but not as a performer."

"Oh, c'mon, sir, we'll join in with you, how would that be?"

The professor let out a huge sigh. "Well, I did warn you," he said with a shrug. Then, in a gravelly baritone he began singing a song which had the tune of "Onward Christian Soldiers":

Lloyd George knew my fa-a-a-ther, Father knew Lloyd George,

Lloyd George knew my father, Father knew Lloyd George.

As he began to run through those immortal lyrics a second time, the Welshmen joined in, embellishing the simple tune with glorious harmonies. This time it brought tears to my eye.

When they finished, everyone gave a rousing cheer.

"Drinks are on me!" Professor Challenger shouted out. His words brought an even louder cheer.

23

The 26th of April proved to be a long, tiring day, but the Caernarvon pub-keeper's prediction about the weather proved accurate. Some sun, no showers, and only a light breeze. We hoofed it on the narrow pilgrims' trails that skirted the northern edge of the peninsula, the Irish Sea always visible on our right. A couple of times we halted for rest breaks in small dark churches along our route. They were quiet, peaceful places exuding sanctity and solemnity. They almost made me feel like a true pilgrim. Mason and Wilkins always approached the small altars and knelt down in quiet prayer. I found the various objects in some of them— baptismal fonts, traditional rush crosses—fascinating. One of the ancient stone fonts was adorned with a simple but charming bit of Celtic knotwork.

We straggled into Aberdaron just before dusk. The village consisted of nothing more than a few random cottages and a shop or two, all of them huddled in the lee of a high hill to the west. The Ty Newydd Hotel was where we arranged to lay our weary heads. It was the final stop for most pilgrims before making the crossing to the island. The proprietor said he would arrange our passage with a local fisherman, a man well acquainted with the treacherous currents between the tip of the peninsula and Ynys Enlli.

From the village we had no sight of the island, though we could see a couple of other, smaller ones off to the southeast, the St. Tudals.

My father-in-law, who'd always been a most vigorous campaigner, was no longer a young man, and when we all sat down to our evening meal, he looked all-in. The doctor and Lord Roxton, a pair of fit middle-aged men, had made the hike look like child's play, as I'd expected. But it was the reverend and the banker who'd impressed me the most. They were the ones whose fitness I'd been worried about, but they'd completed the trek without complaint. In the end, they certainly looked quite spent, but all in all, they'd held up surprisingly well. As for me, I don't mind saying that I was knackered. I longed for a draft of moist and corny ale, as Geoffrey Chaucer might say, but I stuck to my guns and drank only lemonade. I couldn't tell you why.

About eleven o'clock, feeling restless, I wandered out to the beach. The moonless night sky was bright and star-filled, the sound of the waves sliding up over the sandy beach soothing. My body felt achy and weary, but I was excited. Now, only an hour or so away across the water lay Ynys Enlli, our goal. We should be getting there tomorrow, winds and tides permitting.

I was staring in that direction when I perceived the dark outline of a figure coming towards me on the beach. I knew it couldn't be my father-in-law, for he'd been deeply asleep when I slipped from our room, and once GEC was down for the count, he was down for the count. The reverend, the doctor, and Lord John Roxton had been engrossed in a card game in the hotel lounge, so that left only Wilkins.

"Hello, Ted," came McCauley's voice. "Surprised you're still up."

"Felt the need for a little beach stroll," I said. "As if we haven't walked enough for one day."

He gave a low chuckle. "If you prefer solitude, I'll leave you to it."

"No, happy to have your company—and also to have a chance to offer you an apology."

"Whatever for?"

"That little joke I played on you at the castle, McCauley. I'll admit it was rather mean-spirited. I'm sorry I alarmed you."

"Well, Ted, you certainly did. But I'm thinking that I may have overreacted. For some time now my emotions have been quite—what's the word? —fraught? Perhaps you know why."

"The death of your wife, I'd imagine."

"Ted, my wife didn't just die, she was *murdered*."

"*Murdered?* Gosh sakes, that I didn't know. Must've occurred when I was off gallivanting about in Scotland. I am so sorry. I hope, at least, they've caught the perpetrator."

"No, they haven't. At first they thought it was me."

I didn't say anything in response to that. I didn't want him to know I had more knowledge of the matter than I was letting on. Both the professor and I believed that McCauley had been deeply involved in his wife's demise in one fashion or another and that he was being tormented more by guilt than by grief.

"But," he went on, "they changed their tune when they studied the matter more fully."

"Well, good. So you've come on this adventure in hopes of . . . ?"

"In hopes of finding greater peace of mind. Not my idea, really, but the Reverend Mason's. Ted, I believe you and I and Professor Challenger have one important thing in common, we've all lost our spouses fairly recently, right?"

"It was the Spanish Flu that took Jessica, my mother-in-law. Enid, my wife, died in that big London tram collision."

"Ah, terrible business, both of those things."

"I was devastated by Enid's tragic death. I'd like to think I've gotten beyond my initial stage of grief, but I'm not certain of that. Remember the conversation we had back on the train about human emotions? You said you thought grief was the hardest one. I tend to agree with you. It's the roughest thing I've ever experienced. Anyway, how are you holding up?"

"Not good. An hour doesn't go by that I don't think of her."

In the darkness I couldn't make out his face clearly, but his voice told me his misery was genuine.

We stood there without speaking for a while. Finally he said, "Ghosts, Ted. Do you believe in them?"

I pondered his question before offering an answer. "Hmm. Well, I have had a few experiences which some folks might think involved ghosts. I'm not sure about that. I do believe, though, that each of us possesses a spiritual essence, one that continues in some fashion or another after our physical bodies are gone. Residual psychic energy, if you like. That's the way Dr. Atkinson would probably put it."

"Heaven and hell?"

"Ah. Don't know about that. Maybe in one sense or another. Speaking of hell, McCauley, are you familiar with the Orpheus legend?"

"Only vaguely. A musician, wasn't he?"

"About the best harpist there ever was. When the King of the Underworld abducted his wife, he went in search of her and used his playing to charm Cerberus, the three-headed hound who served as gatekeeper to the Land of the Dead. Then he used his music to charm the King of the Underworld, too. As a reward, the King granted him whatever he most desired. Of course, what he desired was to have his wife back. The King reluctantly agreed but with a condition."

"Ah, yes, no looking at her until they'd reached the mortal world."

"Exactly. But he couldn't do it. He *had* to look at her. He couldn't help himself. So he lost her forever."

"Sometimes we just can't help ourselves, eh, Ted? Bring about our own tragedies."

"Yes, sometimes we do."

For a long moment neither of us spoke. "Would you do it, Ted?" he asked me. "Would you risk going into the land of the dead if you thought there was a chance you could retrieve your lost wife?"

I took a minute to reflect on his question. "McCauley," I said at last, "I can't say that I know the answer to that question. I'd like to say that I would risk it. But in all honesty, I just don't know."

24

It was late morning before the fisherman thought the sea was calm enough to attempt the crossing to the island.

"Ain't no sense in takin' chances," he said. "This bit o' water's spelled doom for quite a few rash fellas. I don't aim ta be one o' 'em." Professor Challenger nodded his agreement. McCauley Wilkins, looking jittery, bounced back and forth from one foot to the other. Lord John looked impassive, as usual. I was eager to get going, but not so eager as to want to risk my neck.

"An old Jewish wise man once told me," Challenger declared, "that before you set out to sea you should always say one prayer. Before you fly in an aeroplane you should say two prayers. And before you wed, you should say three prayers. I suggest we reverse that adage and say three prayers now. Reverend Mason, would you like to do the honors?"

We all knew my father-in-law was being droll, but Mason obliged anyway. "Almighty Father, who divided the dry land from the oceans, who parted the Red Sea so the Children of Israel could safely cross, and who calmed the Sea of Galilee so our Lord could walk upon it—if it be Thy will, grant us a safe crossing this day to the holy island." His three short prayers concluded, we all chorused "amen."

We clambered into the boat, which seemed quite small to me. There was a single large sail near the front of the boat and a tiller near the rear. The six of us plopped ourselves down on wooden benches snugged up against the sides of the open boat. A small auxiliary outboard motor was fitted onto the stern of the boat. "An ounce of prevention," the man told us proudly. "We're not likely to need it today, though," he said. Beneath the benches were life jackets and oars, should we need them. The fisherman gave us yellow oilskins to protect ourselves against the flying sea spray.

The wind and waves had become reassuringly calm, but the cool air was filled with sea mist. I think we all felt a good bit of anxiety, knowing how unpredictable the currents surrounding Ynys Enlli were said to be.

The wind filled the sail and propelled us forward, the boatman handling the tiller deftly. The boat nosed out into the gray-blue sea, and it wasn't long until the little village of Aberdaron had disappeared into the mist behind us.

As we proceeded the boat took on a rocking motion. I hoped Wilkins wouldn't get seasick, but as it turned out it was the Reverend Mason who, ten minutes into our journey, was spewing his breakfast over the side. After he'd lurched back to his seat, I saw that he looked distinctly green about the gills.

We endured the rigors of that nerve-racking boat trip for another forty-five minutes before the fisherman looked back at us and pointed off to the west. A shape had appeared on the horizon. At first I wondered if it was it a whale but soon realized it was our goal. As the outline of the island became clearer, I saw that it was bulbous on one end and on the other it tapered off to a narrow line just rising above the sea. As we got nearer, I could see there was a tower poking up on the hillside on the island's rounded end and a lighthouse rising up at about the mid-point on the flattish end.

Eventually the fisherman pointed the prow toward the land and we coasted silently in to the little jetty. The sea mist had cleared and we had our first real look at the island. It didn't look like anything special. In the next few days, I was to learn otherwise.

We were met by a very large chap encased in a shapeless brown cassock. On his chest hung a large wooden pectoral cross.

"Welcome, my friends," he called out, "welcome to our holy sanctuary. I am Brother Anthony, and I shall direct you to the pilgrims' hostel."

We muttered our hellos and introduced ourselves.

"By coming here you are submitting yourselves to the capricious elements of wind and wave," he said. "There are real dangers and uncertainties in such an exposed environment. But I suspect you wouldn't be here if that wasn't part of the island's allure."

"Might I ask," the Reverend Mason asked him, "what religious affiliation you may have?"

"Sir, I am a Christian. Here we recognize no distinctions amongst the denominations, only the broad categories of religions. All who come here are welcome whether they are Christians or not. Most are. At the moment, there are no Jews, Moslems, Buddhists, or Hindus on the island, but they do sometimes turn up, and they are always welcome. We also sometimes have pilgrims who adhere to some of the world's most ancient beliefs, beliefs that elude or defy easy classification. All who come respectfully to this holy place are welcome. What most of us, and most of our visitors, have in common is a deep reverence for the life spiritual. I hope that is true for all of you as well."

With Wilkins trailing along slowly behind us, his face bearing the look of a dazed quail, Brother Anthony led us along a broad pathway to the rough-looking wooden structure that served as the pilgrims' hostel. He told us it had once been a stable. The rough plank walls inside the building were lined with primitive bunks, more like narrow cots than beds. "Take your pick," he said. "At the moment you are our only guests, and it's likely to remain that way. Few pilgrims come before June, and you are here even before the beginning of May. I wonder if there is any special reason for that?" he said aloud, with lifted eyebrows. None of us responded to his question. "Well, whatever the reason, you are welcome."

The building had just two large windows in the eastern wall. They provided the only light and a glimpse of the far-off coast of Wales. There were no windows on the western, or seaward, side. Brother Anthony proudly showed us the brand-new Aga stove just imported from Sweden that sat in the center of the room, the room's only source of heat, its stovepipe poking up through the ceiling. "We will provide you with tea, bread, and eggs for your breakfast, which you must make for yourselves. There is no mid-day meal. The monastery where we live is half a mile away, just beyond the ruins of the medieval abbey. You need only follow the path toward the high hill. You are welcome to join us there if you wish for our evening meal which we serve at six—our fare is simple but hearty. We hold regular services in the chapel each evening at seven. You are welcome to join us whenever it suits you, but you are not obliged to."

"I shall look forward to joining you," the Reverend Mason said firmly, his face still tinged with green.

"The few farmers on the island are accustomed to our having pilgrims here, but we would ask that you stay clear of their crops and do not trouble their sheep. Life is not easy on this little island, not for the farmers, not for us, and not for the pilgrims who come. That is one of the reasons why the first monks came and one of the reasons why we are here now."

"Is there a cemetery?" Challenger asked the man.

"No, not as such, though there are some graves close beside the Tower of St. Mary. 'The Island of the 20,000 Saints' is something of a misnomer, but there's no doubt that a very great number of our predecessor monks are indeed buried here. Whenever and wherever we dig, we encounter their remains. Many ancient kings and nobles are believed to have been buried here as well, wanting their final resting place to put them in the company of the most holy.

"You may have encountered the rumor that Merlin is buried here. That notion seems rather fanciful to me, but who knows? I tend to prefer the legend that Merlin is not dead but lives on in a kind of eternal captivity to atone for his deeds.

"Well, sirs, once again I say welcome. Please do join us for our evening meals and our services, if you wish to."

25

After Brother Anthony departed, we took a few minutes to choose our beds and settle in to this truly humble abode. "Think I'll just have a lie-down," Challenger said. "Still feeling the effects of yesterday's hike."

"I think I'll wander on up to the other end of the island and have a look at the remains of the medieval abbey," I said.

"I'll come with you, Ted," Lord John said.

"Mind if I come as well?" Wilkins asked.

The three of us set off, leaving the other three behind. Dr. Atkinson thought it wise for him to keep an eye on both the reverend, who was still looking sickish, and my father-in-law, who'd been feeling a little faint.

Following the path that bisected the island lengthwise, we set off toward the high hill, and it took us a quarter of an hour to make our way up and over the shoulder of the hill known as "Bardsey Mountain"—a sizeable hill but hardly a mountain—to where the remains of the medieval monastery were located. On our way we passed a few fields, some recently plowed but not yet under cultivation, some with young crops just now poking though the soil; a few small flocks of sheep; and a scattering of houses and farm buildings, most of them having a well or a spring nearby. There should be no shortage of drinking water on the island, I thought, so no impediment to us having our morning cups of tea.

The monastic complex was snugged up against the middle slopes on the leeward side of the hill. There were several terraces above it and another one below it. The buildings were mostly dilapidated and uninhabitable except for the monks' dormitory and refectory, which were just beyond the medieval complex. They had been erected in the nineteenth-century, when the medieval chapel had also been restored. In the midst of the medieval complex rose the thirteenth-century tower of St. Mary, which looked quite ruinous. Nearby stood an impressive pair of Celtic crosses, also erected in the nineteenth century.

From the terrace just above us, I could hear sounds made by people hoeing and raking the earth. The monks were preparing for their spring planting, no doubt. One of them, having become aware of our presence, came down to speak with us.

"Welcome," he said, "I am Brother Fergus." He was a tall thin man with a weather-beaten face and close-cropped gray hair, hair that still bore a reddish tinge. "I'm guessing you've just arrived."

"Quite right," I said. We introduced ourselves, and he offered to show us about the ruins of the monastic complex. He'd obviously done this many times, for he anticipated most of our questions before we could ask them.

"How long have you been on the island?" Lord John asked him.

"Going on twenty years," he replied. "That makes me the second longest inhabitant, after Brother Anthony, who's been here since time immemorial."

"You must like it here," Roxton said.

He laughed. "I guess you could say that. Living on this tiny, isolated island offers a great many challenges, not the least of which is living in a small, self-contained society of cantankerous men. It's no bed of roses. But none of us came here looking for a bed of roses. No, it's a hard but good life here. I suspect it's as free from the corruption of the world as any place on earth. Those of us who choose to stay here live in harmony as best we can, with each other and with nature. I'd say we do pretty well, too."

"You are a Christian?" I asked.

Brother Fergus hesitated for a moment before replying. "Nominally, I guess I am," he finally admitted. "I admire Christianity and I agree with most of its tenets. But I also subscribe to some more ancient beliefs, beliefs that I share with my Celtic forebears."

"With your Celtic forebears? My word," I said. "This is surely not the right moment, but I would like to hear more about your beliefs before we leave the island."

"Anything special you want me to swot up on?"

"Beltane. I'd like you to tell me all about this upcoming Celtic holy day."

Brother Fergus rubbed his hand over his chin. "Ah," he said at last. "And how much longer do you suppose your group will be staying here?"

"About a week, I think."

"Ah, excellent. Then you'll be staying here longer than most of our visitors do. Should give us plenty of opportunity to chat about Beltane. And, as a matter of fact, you'll be here at just the right time to experience it." He grinned at me. "I think, Mr. Malone, you must truly be an Irishman at heart, though you look and speak like an Englishman. I can sense that you're a man who feels a kinship with our ancient beliefs."

"Perhaps I do," I said. "We shall see, I guess."

"The tower," Wilkins said, pointing at the nearby structure. "Are we permitted to climb it?"

"It's not recommended," Brother Fergus replied, "though we don't prohibit it. It's quite dangerous, actually. There are some gaps where portions of the steps have fallen away, gaps which you will need to leap over in order to proceed upward. Also, there are no guardrails anywhere though there is an old iron handrail on the outside wall beside the steps. The tower was erected over an ancient souterrain dug into the hillside long before the Middle Ages. There's an open shaft down the center of the tower that extends all the way down to the souterrain, so one must stay close to the outer walls when braving the tower steps. It's not *too* difficult in dry weather.

"I have to admit that when you get to the top you have a fine view of the south coast of the peninsula. On a clear day, you even get a magnificent view of the high mountains of North Wales. But again, do not ever try climbing the tower after a rainstorm. Those old stone steps would be far too treacherous. Once, maybe five years ago, a foolish pilgrim did and plunged to his death."

"Goodness," I said.

"And what about the lighthouse we could see from the boat?" Wilkins asked. "Is climbing it permitted?"

"The lighthouse keeper will enjoy showing it to you. He's a proud man. But you can't go in without his permission."

"I understand," Wilkins replied.

"Well, I'd best get back to the gardening, or the others will be accusing me of being a shirker."

After Brother Fergus returned to the terrace above us, Lord John said, "I shall be leaving you now and returning to the hostel to check on our invalids. Give Atkinson a breather."

I nodded my agreement. "I'm going to explore a bit more," I said.

After Lord John departed, it was just me and Wilkins who remained there.

"How about we give the tower a try?" he said. "Should be nice and dry so the steps won't be too slippery right now."

"Not much wind, either. So, yes, I'm game," I said.

I was impressed by the interest our "wee, sleekit, timorous beastie" had in the tower. But I certainly hadn't anticipated him wanting to *climb* it. I figured he was far too faint of heart. Maybe Wilkins had more mettle than I'd given him credit.

"McCauley," I said, "I won't play any jokes on you this time, I promise."

He gave me a dubious look, then nodded.

There's a strange appeal to climbing towers. Why that is I'll leave to the psychologists. Maybe Jung's collective unconscious comes into it in some fashion. Anyway, it would certainly be a good way to have a view of the entire island, never mind the frisson of excitement and danger towers offer.

Just as Brother Fergus had warned us, the stone steps were badly eroded by years of harsh weather, but with care we inched our way upward. There was an old iron hand rail attached to the external wall that provided some support though it was quite corroded in places. We discovered that there were three levels in the tower with small landings when we reached the second and third tiers. In the center of each landing was the open shaft Brother Fergus had told us about.

When we reached the top we found a small flat open space only partly protected by a low stone parapet that had crumbled away in spots. We weren't really very high up, maybe just sixty or seventy feet, but it certainly seemed like we were. I wouldn't want to be standing there in a stiff wind.

The open shaft down to the souterrain didn't extend this far up and Wilkins nervously stepped out into the center of the small space. I came and stood beside him, not eager to get too close to the edge.

"Gosh," he said, "you really do get a good view of the mountains from here. 'Majestic' is the word that comes to mind."

I could see the island in its entirety and also the whole extent of the southern coast of the peninsula, beyond which rose the mighty peaks of Snowdonia. "I can't argue with 'majestic,'" I said.

"Ted," he asked me in a soft but serious voice, "do you hear it?"

"Hear what?"

"The voice."

"The voice?"

"The little voice inside your head saying 'Jump!'"

I knew what he was talking about.

"Don't listen to that little imp, McCauley." The word imp, which I uttered without thinking, brought to my mind the little stone demon McCauley had spent so much time studying at Chester Cathedral.

"If we were to jump," he said, "maybe we could join our wives."

"And maybe we would just smash our hips and ribs and live the rest of our lives as helpless crippled invalids."

"You're a spoilsport, Ted. Besides I'm not really serious about jumping. But I do hear that little voice."

"Actually, McCauley, I hear it as well."

We stood there for a few more minutes without speaking as we drank in the impressive view.

"Really worth it, " he said at last. "Well, shall we go down?"

Wilkins, moving rather sprightly, led the way as we began our descent. When he came to the first gap in the steps he leapt across it with ease. But as his feet landed on the lower step, they skidded on some loose rubble and his body tumbled forward. He grabbed at the iron hand rail on the outer wall, and it came loose in his hand. Now he was hanging out over the open central shaft, still gripping a portion of the iron railing which hadn't come fully unattached from the outer wall.

I managed to clear the gap without misfortune, though I wasn't sure what I could do to assist him.

He was clinging to the broken iron railing with one hand, the other end of the railing still attached to the wall—but how long that would last was anybody's guess.

I dropped to my knees on the step closest to where he was hanging out over the central shaft and reached for his free arm. I managed to clasp his arm just below his elbow. Then the small section of iron railing broke free from the wall, and the whole weight of McCauley's body was now on my one arm. When he let loose of the broken rail, it clanked its way down to the lower depths of the shaft, and I reached my other arm towards his now free arm. I was able to grip it in the same fashion as the first arm, and I found some purchase for my feet around a stone column supporting the upper steps.

McCauley's whole body hung over the open space, supported entirely by my arms. My own body was anchored only by my legs and feet which I had wrapped about the stone column. My shoulders and torso now extended out into yawning void as I clutched Wilkins. Fortunately, he wasn't a large or heavy man, no more than eight or nine stone. Had he been twelve or thirteen, I'd have had no chance of holding him. Nonetheless, both my arms and feet were rapidly tiring. I couldn't do this for much longer. If I didn't drop him, in the next few seconds we would both be plunging to our deaths.

"Let go, Ted," I heard him whisper. "Drop me."

McCauley's body was swaying just slightly back and forth above the opening. The thought suddenly struck me that if I could increase that movement, maybe I could swing him closer to the steps. I used my last bits of strength in an attempt to achieve more of a pendulum movement of his suspended body. One swing, two swings, three swings.

McCauley threw one of his legs up onto the steps.

"Try to grab the iron handrail again," I gasped.

I let go of his arm as he reached for it, and I felt myself being pulled into the abyss by the weight my other arm was trying to support. I *had* to let go, there was no other choice.

Miraculously, Wilkins managed to clutch onto a secure section of the iron handrail and the blasted thing held firmly to the outer wall. In the next moment, he was hoisting himself onto the stone steps. When he'd succeeded in doing that, he lay there with closed eyes and heaving chest.

After all the weight was off of my arms and my legs, they remained in an agony of pain. I too lay sprawled out on the steps just a little above Wilkins, trying not to think about what had nearly happened. But the terror lingered, and I found myself shivering.

We must have just lain there like that for the next five minutes.

"Ted," he finally said. "I just learned something."

"What's that?" I gasped breathily.

"That I don't wish to die."

"Did you have some uncertainty about that?"

"I did, Ted. I don't any longer." I made no reply. "Ted, I very nearly killed you. I am so glad that I didn't."

Me, too, I thought, me too.

This conversation was making me uncomfortable. For I knew that when the situation had reached the crisis point and I must either drop him or die along with him, I was going to take the first option. It was only by a miracle that another option presented itself.

After a few more minutes, the two of us descended wordlessly. It was no easy matter to collect one's wits after such an occurrence, and I suddenly felt a desperate need to be alone. I think McCauley must have felt the same way, for we parted in silence and went our separate ways.

My plan was to ascend to the island's highest point and the splendid isolation offered atop Mt. Bardsey. I didn't think it would be an especially long or arduous climb. And as I was trudging upward, I saw that McCauley was doing the opposite, working his way down to the island's shoreline. I guess he wanted to wander alone along the little bays and rocky inlets.

Despite not wanting to think about what had just happened in the tower, I couldn't prevent my thoughts from returning there. It was my actions in the tower when McCauley slipped on the steps and slithered out into the open shaft that caused me consternation. Without even thinking, I'd simply reacted in my attempt to save him. That was a natural thing, one that most people would have done, I thought. It wasn't so much a conscious choice as a normal human response. Then, when it appeared that I wouldn't be able to save him, I did make a conscious choice. I decided to let go of him so that I wouldn't share his fate. That was an exercise of my own free will, not an unconscious reaction.

But despite my intentions, *something* intervened, something had overridden my own choice, my own free will. Was it simply by random chance that my intentions had been thwarted? Or was it because of divine providence? Or was it, perhaps, due to some other spiritual force for which I had no name?

One thing was certain, I thought, as I slowly ascended the steep hillside—that terrifying event in the tower had surely cost me, Ted Malone, one of my nine lives. I couldn't help wondering how many of them still remained. I knew I'd used up at least two or three of them in The Lost World, so maybe I had four or five remaining, I wasn't sure. That seemed like a safe and solid number—though I knew how quickly they could be expended.

Then I remembered how the little girl Rosie claimed her witch-cat, Graymalkin, had put a spell on me. Was that what caused our predicament? Or maybe it hadn't been an evil spell, as I'd assumed, but a *good* spell. Maybe *that's* what saved our lives inside the tower. Such a ridiculous notion caused me to smile.

Gazing from atop Bardsey Mountain I could make out the hazy outline of the entire island. I saw the little group of monks who were working the land on the terrace several hundred yards below me; then down on the lower-lying agriculture section of the island I saw the lighthouse. Maybe half a mile away I spotted a small figure making his way along the island's eastern shore. No doubt it was McCauley

Wilkins, though from this distance I couldn't be sure. I imagined that he was as lost in his jumbled-up thoughts as I had been.

I raised my eyes and saw that I now had an even more dramatic view of the peaks of Snowdonia than I'd had from atop the tower. Suddenly I thought of a verse from the Psalms: "I will lift up my eyes unto the hills, from whence cometh my help. My help cometh from the Lord, which made heaven and earth." Could that have been who intervened back in the tower?

26

McCauley Wilkins, *after parting from Ted Malone, found a little trail that led him down to a rocky outcrop along the island's southern-most tip, a place where wind and waves constantly pounded the rough, rocky shore. He stood for a while on a ledge overlooking the sea, allowing the sea mist to soak his hair and drip down his face. "Thou anointest my head with oil," he whispered to himself, "my cup runneth over." McCauley knew that he had recently experienced a walk through the valley of the shadow of death. If it had been the Lord who'd intervened on his behalf, through the agency of Ted Malone, he wondered why. In his mind he surely didn't deserve it. Was the Lord giving him a chance, in what remained of his life, to atone for his mistakes and misdeeds?*

After a few minutes, he left the ledge and followed the shoreline along the eastern side of the island. Here the going proved much easier than on the rugged, rocky western side.

Here he encountered vast colonies of seabirds, including puffins and shearwaters, and even a sandy cove inhabited by a group of grey seals.

After moving a goodly distance along the eastern shore, ahead of him he spotted a bright patch of whiteness. As he drew nearer he could see that it was a blossoming tree. A hawthorn, perhaps? No, it wasn't. It turned out to be—of all things—a gnarled old apple tree, dappled with pink and white blossoms. How lovely it was! Although McCauley had encountered some impressive things on this remote little isle, few of them could be called lovely. But the apple tree, with its myriad blossoms, truly was. He would try to remember to ask the brothers for more information about the apple tree.

McCauley ended his meanderings just short of the lighthouse, which he decided not to visit. He'd had his fill of climbing to high places for one day. Indeed, perhaps he'd had his fill for a lifetime. He tried to keep his thoughts away the near fatal disaster in the medieval tower, but they kept returning there anyway. How fortunate he'd been that Ted Malone had come to his rescue. He'd had mixed feelings about Malone, but the fellow hadn't hesitated to come to his aid and risk his own life in the process. He felt a profound gratitude toward Ted, gratitude that canceled out any other reservations he might have about the young journalist.

27

The monks' refectory was a long narrow room, a sturdy wooden table running down the middle. Backless benches sat on each side. Half a dozen unlit-candles were spaced out down the middle of the table and wooden trenchers and large tankards lay similarly spaced out on each side. At the far end of the room a door to the kitchen area stood open, and sounds and smells of food preparation emanated from that small room.

"Welcome, friends," said Brother Anthony, coming through the kitchen door into the main part of the room. He waved us toward the two empty benches on the left side of the refectory table. "You are right on time. I am so pleased that you've all come. The sea air does stir one's appetite, eh? I hope you had a restful afternoon and will enjoy some spritely conversation with us this evening as we dine."

I wouldn't have called my afternoon's activities restful.

But they'd been stimulating, not to say downright unnerving. I glanced at McCauley, whose eyes darted briefly in my direction, before returning to Brother Anthony's face.

"Our evening fare is always simple but ample," Brother Anthony went on. "Believing that one should not live by bread alone we always provide a dish or two in addition to our baskets of bread. Tonight Brother Aled, the best cook amongst us, has prepared a thick and savory stew. It's one of his specialities and one of my own personal favorites. I hope it will be to your liking also."

The outside door, the one by which we'd entered, now came open again and the little group of brothers trooped in. There were five of them and they arranged themselves on the benches across from us. They gave us acknowledging nods, and after each of them had named himself, we did also. I had only taken a momentary glance at them earlier when they'd been tilling the soil in their garden, so now I took a moment to study them more closely.

The one who called himself Liam was a sandy-haired, red-faced Irishman with sparkling blue eyes and a ready grin. It turned out that he was the one monk amongst them with a sense of humor. To me, he was probably the most likeable of the whole bunch.

Fergus, the monk who'd showed us about earlier and who was reputed to be an expert on ancient Celtic lore, was a tall, thin, serious-minded fellow. He'd been gregarious when he'd been with us, but in the presence of the other monks he was unexpectedly quiet. I got the sense that he was something of an outlier within the group.

Brother Thomas, who turned out to be their master gardener, was a stocky, round-shouldered cove with a bulbous nose and several extra chins. He made me think of Friar Tuck from the Robin Hood tales. I think he had fairly limited interest in anything other than plants.

The most educated and intellectual of them was Brother Adelard, a name he'd chosen for himself after the medieval scholar Adelard of Bath. He'd once been a professor of Biblical Studies at Edinburgh University, and later we learned that when he'd become disillusioned by the jealousies and hypocrisies that flourish in the academic world, he'd sought a life of greater purity and simplicity here on Ynys Enlli. Here he was left alone to study and contemplate to his heart's content.

The shyest and quietest of them was named Brother Malachi. Aside from telling us his name, he never spoke another word the whole evening other than "amen." He sat placidly amidst his fellow monks, who paid him scant attention. He had strikingly large, greenish-brown eyes and a pair of jug ears so large I could have picked him up by them. A small cherubic smile was displayed upon his innocent-looking mug, and he appeared to be entirely lost in a world of his own. He was a good illustration of a person my grandmum would have called "fey." In some respects, he struck me as the most unworldly, not to say otherworldly, of the whole bunch. Later, Professor Challenger said to me that he believed Brother Malachi to be "the most blissful little pixie in the entire forest." Maybe, I thought, that wasn't such a bad thing to be.

Brother Anthony carried in three large baskets filled with large hunks of bread, and close behind him came Brother Aled holding a large pot of stew, the rich, savory smell of which filled the room. He motioned for us, the guests, to send our wooden trenchers in his direction. Holding a large ladle in one hand and Mason's empty trencher in the other, he looked at the Reverend and said, "Bach or mawr?"

"A little or a lot," Challenger whispered to the Reverend. Mason sang out, "Bach, please," and Aled spooned in a modest portion and passed the plate back.

That process went on for a couple of minutes until all the men's plates had been served. Then everyone rose to their feet as Brother Anthony intoned simply, "For what we are about to receive, we are truly grateful."

"Amen," chorused all the men, including the otherwise silent Brother Malachi.

Brother Aled hurried back to the kitchen area and then returned holding two large pitchers of cider. The sight of them caused the monks to smile. One of them contained a potent variety of scrumpy-jack, the other a sparkling variety of non-alcoholic apple juice. As the pitchers were passed around, most of the men eagerly poured the scrumpy into their tankards. But Brother Adelard, I noticed, chose the plain apple juice. So did the Reverend Mason, McCauley Wilkins, and me. Seeing that I'd chosen the plain juice, a grinning Brother Liam said, "I thought you were an Irishman, Mr. Malone."

"Must be an Orangeman," Brother Fergus said, "one o' them Scotch Proddies who've long been intrudin' upon our fair land." I didn't mind their good-natured joshing.

The breadbaskets were passed round, each man helping himself to one or two large pieces of bread. Then, all at once, everyone tucked in. I soon discovered that the thick stew consisted mostly of vegetables—potatoes, carrots, onions, rutabagas, and a few others I couldn't identify; there was only a small amount of meat, which I guessed to be mutton. The stew was heavily spiced, almost to excess but not quite.

For the first few minutes there was almost no conversation. Then Brother Anthony looked across at us and said, "I'm sure you have many questions for us, about our lives and our work here, perhaps about the island itself, perhaps about matters of theology or spirituality. Please don't hesitate to ask us. We are at your disposal, to the extent that our combined wisdom allows."

None of us spoke up right away, but it was McCauley Wilkins who finally did. "In my wanderings today," he said, "I came upon a beautiful apple tree that was in full blossom. I don't know much about trees, apple trees or any others, but I was surprised. I wouldn't have guessed there would be an apple tree growing out here on this remote island."

"It is quite miraculous," Brother Thomas, the chief gardener, said. "No one knows how the ancient tree came to be here, but it, and likely its predecessors, have survived here on the island for quite some time. In fact, cuttings from it have been used to propagate other trees in vineyards throughout Britain. We are proud to say that the 'Bardsey Apple' has become quite a prized variety of apple."

"Interesting," mumbled Challenger.

"Were apples from that tree used to make this cider?" Dr. Atkinson asked.

"Oh, no," replied Brother Thomas. "Not a sufficient yield to do that, though we do greatly cherish the ones we collect to eat. Aled has made some wondrous pies from them as well."

"I have indeed," the cook's face beamed with pride as he rubbed his stomach with his right hand.

"Perhaps your tree is descended from the one in the Garden of Eden," Professor Challenger said, I assumed facetiously.

"This *is* our Eden," Brother Adelard replied seriously, "though it's far less hospitable than the real Eden, I feel rather sure. But sir, I must take exception to your last statement. There is nothing in the Scriptures to indicate that the Tree of Knowledge in the Garden of Eden was an apple tree; or that Eve tempted Adam with an apple. Those are common but erroneous suppositions."

"I bow to your erudition," my father-in-law said, with an

acknowledging nod.

"Aren't apples and apple trees quite important in Celtic mythology?" I asked. I remembered reading about them in the research I'd done in Dr. Williams's Library in London. Brother Liam and Brother Malachi both nodded their agreement with my question, then looked expectantly at Fergus, whom they recognized as the resident expert on all things Celtic.

"Quite right," he said. "Well, Malone, perhaps you are an Irishman after all."

"Mind elaborating?" Challenger queried.

"Not at all. Apples, as you may or may not know, are closely associated with the number five, a number that was venerated in Celtic lore. After the number three, five is perhaps the most important one in Celtic numerology. The Celts believed that several of the prime numbers held magical, mysterious significances—especially the numbers three, five, thirteen, and seventeen."

"How is it that apples are associated with the number five?" I asked, wonderingly.

"For one thing," Fergus explained, "each of the blossoms this chap saw today on the Bardsey apple tree, like all apple blossoms, has five petals. For another, there are five seed pockets inside every apple. Cut an apple in half and you will see them. And those seed pockets, if you were to connect them with a drawn line, would form a five-sided figure, a pentagram, an important shape in Celtic lore."

"But beside the fact that five is a prime number," I said, returning the discussion to Celtic numerology, "why did the Celts venerate that number?"

"Many things important to them occur in fives. They believed that there were five elements, not just four: the four traditional ones—air (or wind), fire, earth, and water—but also a fifth element which was the most vital of all: *spirit*. They believed that all things, animate or inanimate, possess a spiritual essence. They saw that reflected throughout nature. They saw it in the apple as well as in the human body which also reflects the number five—with the four limbs and the head making five; and in the human hand, with its four fingers and thumb.

"You probably know how important the spiral was in early Celtic art. The ancient Celts saw the spiral as symbolizing man's spiritual journey in this life and on into the next, and they considered five to be the number of the spiral."

"Umm," said Brother Thomas, dreamily, "can't wait until September when the sweet, sweet apples on that old tree will be ripe once again."

"But," said my father-in-law, "don't you need at least two trees to produce apples. One tree can't pollinate itself, can it?"

"Yes, you certainly do need more than one tree," Thomas replied. "My guess is that bees must fly out from the peninsula to pollinate the new blossoms."

"Is it at all likely they can do that?" Challenger asked in his rumbly voice.

"It *is* rather miraculous, isn't it?" Thomas replied.

"Sounds like the Virgin Birth to me," my father-in-law declared.

Hearing his almost blasphemous comment, all the monks went silent, their faces sober, except for Brother Malachi's, whose mischievous grin remained. It appeared that he alone realized that my father-in-law had a puckish streak.

Finally Brother Anthony said, "Yes, well, as you know, the Lord moves in mysterious ways," a comment that brought the discussion to a close.

"It's drawing toward time for our evening chapel service," Brother Adelard said. "Tonight it is my turn to speak, and my intended subject will be angels."

"Our guests are welcome to join us," Brother Anthony said.

In the end, only McCauley Wilkins and the Reverend Mason took him up on his invitation. The rest of us decided to walk off our evening meal. I, for one, needed a respite from the monks of Ynys Enlli.

28

I awoke in the dawning to the screeching of gulls and the smell of coal smoke from the Aga stove, not to mention the smell of the reverend's pipe. Then I heard humming coming from the direction of Professor Challenger's cot—it sounded like "Mama's little babies love shortnin' bread"—apropos, I suppose, because Dr. Atkinson was heating our scones and preparing our morning tea. A cup of tea and a hot buttered scone with strawberry jam would go down well, I thought. The sea air was probably responsible for my unexpectedly sharp appetite.

Sounds of our companions rousing themselves came from the other cots. Professor Challenger sat up and stretched his arms wide. He looked in my direction, his familiar grin peeping through his thick bush of gray-black whiskers. I smiled back at him as I stretched out my achy arms and shoulders, arms and shoulders that had had an unexpectedly harsh workout yesterday inside that old tower at the monastery.

"I'm feelin' a bit more like my old self this morning, Ted," he declared in his gravelly voice. "If need be, I could set off and explore the swamps of the Lost World."

"No need," came Lord John's voice as he carried a breakfast tray to my father-in-law. "We have been there and done that, and I for one have no burning desire to repeat the experience."

"Much obliged," Challenger said, as he took the tea tray from Roxton and balanced it on his knees. "Mmm, Tetley's finest. Wouldn't be my first choice, but it will have to do. Any port in a storm, as they say."

"Sleep all right, Ted?" my father-in-law asked me. "No nightmares or anything?"

"Slept like the dead," I said, immediately regretting my words. "For the most part, anyway. How about you, sir?"

Challenger ran the fingers of one hand through his thick tangled beard, his head cocked slightly to one side. "Very strange dreams," he muttered at last. "A bit unsettling, to be frank."

Dr. Atkinson, who'd been fussing with the breakfast items on the Aga, swung about and looked at us. "I did as well," he said. Wilkins just stared at all of us wordlessly.

"If your dreams were anything like mine," Lord Roxton said, "you had good reason to find them unsettling. The woman who appeared in my dreams was someone I haven't seen or even thought about in the last twenty years, not since St. Petersburg in '04. The Countess Irina, the luscious little trollop. My word, where in the world did *she* come from?"

"I had a similar experience involving one of my old flames," said Atkinson. "I have to admit it's been a good while since I've had an erotic dream."

"Did she have lustrous dark hair coiled about her head, magnificent blue eyes, smooth white throat and shoulders?" I said with a grin.

"And was she wearing a loose gown of red silk with nothing on beneath it?" added Lord John.

"Her beauty took my breath away," Professor Challenger said, "not a common occurrence at my age. I have to admit, she inspired in me a lust such as I haven't felt in many long years."

"Did you recognize her?" the Reverend Mason asked.

"Her face, to my surprise," Challenger said, "was the face of my wife."

"The face of the woman in my dream was *my* wife as well," Atkinson declared.

"Though nothing else about her was," said Lord John, "if she was one of your old flames."

"What about the woman in your dream, Ted?" Challenger asked me. "What did she look like?"

"Just like the one who's already been described, except that she was my wife, too." I wasn't certain of that, though. She might have been Isabella.

"Mac?" Challenger said to Wilkins. "What about you? Did you experience a dream similar to what the rest of us experienced?"

"No dreams for me," he said, looking down at the floor. I felt sure he was lying. His dream was probably too embarrassing for him to be willing to describe it.

"Reverend?" Challenger said, kindly choosing not to challenge Wilkins's dubious assertion. "How about you?"

"Well, yes," he admitted after a long pause, "I did have a dream similar to what you've been describing. I didn't recognize her face, though." The look on his face told me he was lying also, that he didn't want to admit whose face it had been. Curious, I thought.

"I guess he wasn't looking at her face," said Lord Roxton, his words drawing laughter from several of us.

"I've never heard of such a thing," Challenger said, "a group of people having a nearly identical dream at the same time on the same night. Wondrous strange."

"We were all in the same room," I pointed out. "Perhaps our visitor took advantage of that to visit each of us in turn."

"Visitor?" Wilkins said in a tremulous voice.

"Ever heard of a succubus, McCauley?" I asked.

"Goodness," said Challenger.

"You are referring to the evil female seductress who comes to men during the night?" asked Atkinson.

"Yes, the female counterpart to an incubus," I said.

"Wasn't Merlin's father an incubus?" Challenger asked.

"According to Geoffrey of Monmouth," I replied, "he was, an incubus who seduced a virtuous mortal woman and begat a child on her, that child being Merlin." I had learned that from my studies at Dr. Williams's Library in London when I was boning up on Celtic Mythology.

"What are these creatures, succubus and incubus?" Wilkin asked in the same tremulous voice. "I've never heard of them."

"Again according to the twelfth-century writer Geoffrey of Monmouth," I said, "they are beings who inhabit the realm between the earth and the moon; they aren't angels and they aren't men—they are something *else*."

"The woman who came to me last night," Lord Roxton said, "was certainly not an angel. She was that little Russian minx, Irina, whose remarkable talents I have never forgotten."

"We don't need you to go into detail," Challenger said primly.

"No, you don't," Lord John shot back. "Because you had a very similar experience yourself last night."

At that point it seemed that most of us were ready to move away from any further discussion of this uncomfortable topic. As I munched on my scones and sucked down my cup of tea, there came to my nose the hint of a fragrance, a fragrance other than that of scones or coal smoke or the Reverend Mason's pipe. It was the fragrance of a subtle perfume. It was, I believe, Yardley's English Roses. How strange.

29

"**Ted, why don't** you and I go and take a gander at this famous apple tree, eh?" Challenger said to me. "Wilkins, you want to join us?"

"Thanks, but no," he said. "Going to have a quiet day today. Kind of overdid it yesterday." I think he was still shaken up by our experience in the tower—no surprise there—and perhaps by his dream last night, a dream he hadn't admitted to having.

I had kept my father-in-law in the dark about the experience McCauley and I had in the tower. But being nobody's fool, I think he suspected something untoward had occurred. His antennae were remarkably adept at picking up signs of such occurrences.

It was just a short walk from the pilgrims' hostel to the gnarled old apple tree. It stood only a few hundred yards from the eastern shoreline near an old farm building, and we reached it in ten minutes.

After the two of us had quietly contemplated the tree for a few minutes, Professor Challenger reached up and grabbed a slender branch, then bent it toward him so he could examine the blossoms at closer range.

"Nice subtle fragrance," he said, sniffing. "Five white petals, just like the man said, surrounding a lean yellow stamen. Looks like the blossoms on this tree are arranged in clusters of four. I think that's the typical arrangement. We're in luck today, Ted. We caught them at just the right time. Apple blossoms don't last long. Less than two weeks, normally." Then completely out of the blue, as was his wont, he intoned, "'Like an apple tree among the trees of the wood, So is my beloved among the sons.'"

"King David?" I asked.

"Close. Solomon, actually. *Song of Songs*. I heard those verses recently at a wedding ceremony. Lots of amorous stuff in that book of the Bible."

"Amorous is one word for it," I replied.

We stayed there a few more minutes looking the apple tree over good. The lovely, delicate blossoms bedecking the slender branches offered a striking contrast to the rest of the gnarled old tree. "There's a lesson in what we are seeing, Ted," Challenger declared. "When you get old, don't forget it." I got his drift and offered no comment.

"Sir," I said, "have you noticed any bees?"

"No, not just yet."

"Me, either."

"Must be a case of a virgin birth," he said, a twinkle in his eye. Again I refrained from commenting.

"In Christianity," Challenger said, "apple trees symbolize the continuance of life, among other things, standing for new birth, freshness, and innocence."

"I can see that," I said. "And I like it, just as I like the way the ancient Celts venerated apples and apple trees."

"In a week or two, after all these lovely blossoms will have faded and fallen, tiny new apples will begin to form."

"That's if these blossoms get properly pollinated. Let's hope they do."

"I've heard that the Lord moves in mysterious ways," he said.

"Well, Ted, what say we mosey down to the coast and see if we can't track down those grey seals Mac told us about. Seals are creatures who have always fascinated me. Whenever I see them I can't help feeling an affinity to them."

"Maybe in a previous life you were a selkie, sir," I responded. He gave me a sidelong glance. "Anyway, why don't you set yourself down on a rock like Saint Cuthbert and sing to them to demonstrate your appreciation."

"Ha, ha. Yes, I could, I could—if only I could sing."

"Maybe you aren't Caruso, sir, but your singing isn't so bad."

"Well, okay then, with your endorsement I shall give it

a try. But you must accompany my gravelly bass with your light baritone."

"I shall do it, sir. Our blended voices will surely wow them."

"What should we sing, Ted? How about 'My Bonnie lies Over the Ocean' or that old sea shanty, 'What shall we do with the drunken sailor?'"

"Let's do both."

30

McCauley Wilkins *felt bewildered. He wasn't close to coming to terms with his near-death experience yesterday, and now, on top of that, he'd had a truly bizarre dream last night involving Felicity, a dream in which she'd seduced him and then taunted and berated him.*

Now, with the others having gone off to do whatever it was that they planned to do, McCauley set off also, in his case in a direction opposite to theirs. The path he chose took him through the low-lying farm fields toward the northern-most tip of the island. It also took him close to the lighthouse. He cast a nervous glance in its direction, then trudged on by. He was in no mood to have any more experiences in high, precarious places. He hadn't forgotten the little voice inside his head urging him to jump.

Now looming in his mind was the question, "Why?" Why had Felicity come to him last night? Had the spirit of the dead woman somehow chosen to do that? Or had his own subconscious desires evoked her? Was she a product of Freud's id or Jung's shadow? In any case, it had truly seemed to be her. She had been every bit as alluring last night as she had been in real life. Maybe even more so.

McCauley knew, if he was honest, that in recent months he had wanted to be rid of her. Had he really wanted her dead? It was possible that he did, but he wasn't entirely sure. In any case, now she was. And he knew that if he had wished her dead it was an unforgiveable and sinful desire. While almost falling to his death yesterday, McCauley had rationalized to himself that that had been the price he'd had to pay for that wicked desire. He believed that his terrifying experience in the tower occurred to provide a form of punishment and perhaps atonement. If so, had his rescue been brought about by Divine Providence? Or did he have a guardian angel who'd intervened, a guardian angel who'd used Ted Malone, of all people, as his agent of salvation?

If all of that wasn't confusing enough, why had Felicity come to him like that last night? It had been exhilarating to see her again, but then afterward it was appalling. It was almost as if she were taunting him by showing him what he had lost. Judging from her earlier appearance at the hotel in Caernarvon, it appeared that she placed the blame for her demise on him. Would she now continue to appear and taunt him like that for the rest of his life? If so, he might be better off drowning himself in the River Thames or hurling himself from the top of that high tower.

"Felicity," he'd cried out to her in his dream, "I had nothing to do with your murder. I don't know who did it. I don't know why. I never wanted such a thing to happen."

Of course that remark wasn't strictly true. He had wanted her to be gone from his life. Was the thought father to the deed? Had his own desires, in some perverted way, led directly to his wife's death? Had he planted that desire in the mind of someone else? He knew her well, he'd been aware of her lovers, and he knew how she took a perverse pleasure in manipulating people and playimg them off against each other. Maybe one of them, in a fit of pique or jealousy, had delivered the coup de grâce. It seemed likely. Maybe someone else wanted to be rid of her, too—maybe even more than he had.

He had come to Ynys Enlli, this island of spirits, in the hope of gaining greater understanding, in the hope of achieving emotional relief, and perhaps in the hope of effecting some kind of atonement. So far, all he'd done was muddy his thoughts and feelings even further.

He thought about the Orpheus legend that Ted had brought up a couple of days ago. Was there some way that he, like Orpheus, could gain access to that mysterious Otherworld and attempt to bring her back? Wouldn't that prove to her that he hadn't really wanted her dead, that he really wanted to win back the love she'd once had for him? He, McCauley Wilkins, perform a deed as heroic as those of the great heroes out of ancient legend? He smiled at the absurdity of such a notion.

McCauley Wilkins knew he was mentally grasping at straws. But what else did he have to grasp at?

31

It was now Friday, April 29th, only one more day until Beltane Eve. Again we accepted the monks' invitation to join them for their evening meal. After seeing the apple tree that morning, I'd had apples and apple trees on my mind the whole livelong day. When I'd been studying the old Celtic myths and legends in Dr. Williams's Library in London, I'd come across a captivating tale called *The Voyage of Bran* in which a magic branch of apple blossoms, held by a beautiful otherworldly woman, was of crucial importance. I thought I might ask Brother Fergus to tell us about this yarn while we ate. Since it was a famous old tale, he would surely be familiar with it.

We reached the building just as the monks were trooping in. They took the same seats as the night before and we did, too. Tonight Brother Thomas had the cooking duties, not Brother Aled, and he'd prepared some sort of curried rice dish with little bits of chicken in it. Goodness, I thought, these monks certainly do like their food spicy. I needed to take a bite of bread and a mouthful of apple juice after almost every spoonful of the curry.

Brother Malachi, sitting across from me, had been watching me closely as I coped manfully with the spicy dish, his cherubic grin growing wider all the while. I glared across at him and said, "You aren't you making fun of me, are you?" His grin spread to his widening greenish-brown eyes and he shook his head innocently. "Like fun, you aren't," I said. I took another swig of apple juice and was about to ask Fergus about *The Voyage of Bran* when Wilkins beat me to the punch, broaching a completely different topic.

"Last evening at the service," he said, addressing Brother Adelard, "you had some most informative and fascinating things to say about angels. But one aspect of the topic you didn't touch on was the matter of Guardian Angels. Lately, I've been wondering a lot about them. I know very little about such angels, though I believe there is some scriptural basis for believing in them. Is that correct? I would be grateful for whatever light you could shed on the matter." I noticed that Brother Malachi's eyes momentarily gleamed a bit brighter.

"Guardian Angels?" Brother Adelard responded. "Is there anything in particular that has provoked your curiosity?" I suspected I knew what had provoked Wilkins's curiosity, but I kept my own council.

"Do you think they exist?" McCauley Wilkins asked, not

responding directly to what he'd been asked. "If so, where do they come from? And if so, does everyone have one? I find it all very perplexing."

"You are right about there being scriptural basis for believing in guardian angels. And yes, there are several biblical passages suggesting the existence of both good and bad spirits. The good ones sometimes function as protectors—your guardian angels—and the bad ones as corruptors—devils or demons. Sometimes the passages imply that these helpful spirits are indeed angels. In a place or two there's the implication that the evil spirits may themselves be *fallen* angels."

"Makes me think of Christopher Marlowe's play *Doctor Faustus*," Professor Challenger said, "with its good and bad Angels."

"Could these good and evil spirits," Wilkins asked, "be the spirits of the dearly departed?"

"Ah, an intriguing possibility, isn't it?" Brother Adelard said. "What are these spirits? Where do they come from? Are they heavenly or demonic beings, or both? Are they the spirits of those who have died? Are they something else altogether? Are they the foot soldiers in the eternal struggle between good and evil?"

"I know that all of you are men of great spirituality," I said, "but have any of you here on the island ever experienced encounters with such spirit beings, whether good or evil?" Brother Malachi looked across at me, his eyes filled with wonder, and Brother Fergus darted his eyes back and forth nervously. I think they were both as eager as I was to hear Brother Adelard's response. I wondered what each of them might say if they were asked to make their own responses, but they didn't get that chance.

The one who spoke was Brother Thomas, the chief gardener. "Every day I invoke the aid of the angels to enhance and protect the vegetables in my gardens," he declared. "I sincerely believe they respond positively to my entreaties."

"But have you actually encountered one of them?" I insisted.

"Hmm. Well, I'm not sure. Late one All Hallows Eve I saw a misty figure lurking in my garden, and the next day some of my ripe squashes were missing. Can't say for sure what that was all about, though at the time I ascribed it to some hungry demon." I thought I heard a faint giggle from Brother Malachi. Was he perhaps a midnight squash thief?

"I regularly converse with the Archangel Gabriel," Brother Anthony said, "but I only hear his voice inside my head. I've never encountered him in person, as it were."

"Well," Professor Challenger said, scratching his thick beard, "lots of questions, eh? Maybe in the next several days we'll get one or two of them answered."

I couldn't help noticing the twinkle in my father-in-law's eyes. He didn't believe for a moment what he'd just said. He was as big a skeptic as ever. The only answers he expected were no answers.

Suddenly into the conversational lull I became aware of a new soft voice. "Storm," it said. The speaker was Brother Malachi. This was his first utterance other than naming himself and saying "amen." The other monks, who'd also heard him, became immediately attentive.

"Storm," he said again, "*big* storm." For once there was no mischievous grin on his face. Now his large, greenish-brown eyes looked like saucers. "Big, *big* storm," he said.

32

As we left the monastic complex, I noticed the bank of dark clouds that had loomed up in the southwestern sky. It was moving towards us.

The six of us were soon strung out single file walking quickly along the path leading back to the pilgrims' hostel. With the prospect of a major storm brewing, none of us—not even the Reverend Mason—chose to join the monks for their vespers service. We wanted to be dry when we'd reached the relative safety and comfort of the converted stable.

Lord Roxton stepped out rapidly in the lead and I brought up the rear, McCauley Wilkins just a few meters ahead of me. As I walked behind him, I imagined him in London on his way to his financial offices in the City, sporting a bowler hat and carrying a neatly furled umbrella, though the brolly he might have had need for, considering the approaching storm. McCauley was striding quickly enough to stay close to the reverend, who was just ahead of him. He seemed spry and fit, and it struck me that he must have lost at least a stone of weight since we left London town. I felt certain that I had. Our recent trials and tribulations may have been playing havoc with our minds, but our bodies had been the beneficiaries.

The air temperature was dropping quickly, and the wind had begun to shriek. We were still a few yards shy of the hostel when large cold drops of rain began falling. Standing by the door, Professor Challenger swung about and shouted out, "'Blow winds and crack your cheeks!'"

"Here's a hovel, Nuncle" I said, trying my feeble best to mimic the Fool in *King Lear*. "Get thee inside. 'Tis no night to be out on the moor pitying the poor, naked wretches."

"Would it surprise you to learn, Ted, that I once trod the boards in the role of King Lear?"

"Was that at university?"

"Uh, no. Sixth form. Didn't lead to a career on the stage, I'm happy to confess."

"A tragic loss to the thespian world and the British public," I said, with a straight face.

"Not funny, Ted. I wasn't half bad, you know, even if I am the only one to say so."

Wind and rain lashed the building. The old structure, which had weathered many more storms than a few, groaned and shuddered. Dr. Atkinson lit the tall, thick candles in the pair of hurricane lamps to alleviate the darkness that nearly enveloped us. They cast spooky shadows about the spacious room. Brother Malachi had been right. The island of Ynys Enlli was in for a big storm.

"Did you notice how attentive the other monks were to Brother Malachi's sudden observation?" the professor said.

"Maybe he's empathic or has a reputation for possessing prophetic powers," the reverend said.

"Or maybe he's just more in tune with the natural world than the rest of us are," I said. "Isn't that sometimes the case with the mentally impaired?"

"Who says he's mentally impaired?" Lord Roxton replied. "Maybe he's just a shy fella."

"Ted, did you notice how interested he was in you?" my father-in-law said. "Could hardly keep his eyes off of you."

"I was sitting straight across from him. Who else would he be looking at?"

"No, he really was rather fixated on you, Malone," the doctor said. "I noticed it also."

"Maybe he is just more in tune with the natural world," the reverend said, "and recognized Ted as being more like him than the rest of us."

I resented the reverend's not-so-subtle barb but bit my tongue.

"I think the poor fella was inebriated," McCauley Wilkins said. "Did you notice how much scrumpy he was putting away? I suspect he's just an alcoholic. Living out here on this god-forsaken island has driven these monks to drink."

"All but Brother Adelard," the reverend said.

"Maybe Brother Malachi recognized me as the only pure and spiritually innocent one amongst us," I declared, "and chose not to expend any energy on the rest of you scoundrels."

"Ha, ha," laughed Professor Challenger. "That's you all over, Ted, pure and spiritually innocent."

I extended my arms out from my sides, the palms of my hands turned forward. "Well, yeah," I declared. "Isn't that so obvious it doesn't need saying?"

The building seemed to rock for a moment as a furious gust of wind crashed against it. The hurricane lamps wobbled but didn't tumble over. We were all silent, listening to the sound of the wailing winds, which seemed to be intensifying.

"I hope the old apple tree won't be blown down," McCauley said. "That would be a terrible shame."

"It's pretty well sheltered in the lee of that nearby farmhouse," the professor said. "Like this building, it's probably survived more than its fair share of big blows."

"Hope you are right," McCauley said.

"The blossoms may well be shredded by now, but it's likely that the tiny new apples that are already forming are safe." I found the professor's words reassuring, and I hoped McCauley did also.

I settled in a corner and worked on my notes for the newspaper while the other five played cards. I wondered if we might be visited again tonight by any spiritual emanations, or whatever it was that had manifested itself last night. Given my druthers, I hoped not.

A couple of hours later I was just about to drop off to sleep when I heard the professor humming. It was the old sea shanty, "Blow the Man Down." I could barely make it out against the howling of the wind and the sound of crashing waves, but then I heard him softly chant the words, "Give us some time to blow the man down."

Everyone had settled down for the night. I could hear Wilkins's low snoring. Dr. Atkinson lay in dead silence, presumably sound asleep. Lord Roxton was tossing and turning, maybe hoping for a visitation from that "little Russian minx Irina." The Reverend Mason was still awake; he was down on his knees beside his bunk praying. The professor continued humming. Then I heard him mutter, "I hope this horrid storm won't do any harm to those lovely seals."

For most of the night the rain beat down on the hostel's roof. It was no gentle thrumming. Harsh winds slammed against the outside walls. Sometimes they whistled down the stovepipe, causing the coal ashes in the Aga to flare up brightly for a moment. Eventually, though, I dropped off to sleep just like the others.

For me, at least, there was no visitation from a succubus, nor did I want one. In fact, for me there was no anything. Once I'd fallen asleep I slept the night through without even being awakened by the ferocity of the storm.

When I awoke in the dawning, it had all changed. The world outside the hostel seemed enveloped in silence. No squawking of gulls, no loud sounds of the surf, no sounds coming from my unconscious mates. It was eerie. Then it came to me that today was April thirtieth, Beltane Eve. We were finally reaching the period of time for which we'd come.

I glanced over at the other cots. All present and accounted for—except for one. One of them was unoccupied. *McCauley Wilkins.*

I lay there wondering about the eerie silence. I supposed that in the aftermath of the storm, a dead calm had settled on the island. Perhaps the storm had stunned the natural world outside the hostel into a state of shock from which it had yet to recover. I could just hear the sound of the surf a couple of hundred yards away, but it seemed strangely muted compared to its normal sound.

No cries of seagulls must have been a rarity. Then I heard the sound of the hostel door opening and closing.

Wilkins.

When he saw me sitting up awake and looking at him, a slightly guilty look crept over his face.

"Went to check on the apple tree," he said in a whisper. "I was worried about it."

"Did it come through all right?" I asked.

"It did, it did. Those lovely blossoms were goners, of

course, but no major limbs were down or anything."

"Made of tough stuff. Probably had a lot of experience surviving the elements out here in this exposed place."

"Guess so. It's odd how I've developed a deep affection for that old tree."

"Maybe in a former life you were one of the tree people," I said.

"*Tree* people?"

"Beings who once were rootless wanderers, before they settled down and gave up their peripatetic ways."

"Ted, you're joshing me."

"Yes, I am, though there's lots of myths and magical stuff involving trees in the Celtic and Germanic mythologies. There's even an old Welsh poem, I think, called something like 'The Battle of the Trees.' And you probably remember the prophecy in *Macbeth* about Birnam Wood coming to Dunsinane Hill."

"Uh, no, can't say I do."

My *Macbeth* reference suddenly caused me to think of the little girl Rosie and her cat Graymalkin, the name of the witch's cat in Shakespeare's play. Rosie claimed her witch-cat had placed a spell on me. Could that be what caused the storm? Hah, what a load of stuff and nonsense, as the professor would say.

"Good morning, gents," came the professor's voice from his cot. "Looks like we survived the night. And what a night it was. I dreamed we were in the Lost World, Ted, listening all night to the jungle drums a-beating away. Didn't make for a restful sleep. All safe and accounted for around here, though, eh?"

"Far as I know. McCauley went to check on the apple tree. Says it came through all right."

"Nice to hear, Mac," the professor said. "Seems like you've developed a rather proprietary interest in that old tree."

"It's a special tree, Professor. A remarkable tree."

"Quite right."

Lord Roxton's head popped up in his cot. "I'll take two spoonfuls of sugar in my tea, please, when you have it ready," he said to no one in particular. "Scones lightly buttered, lots of marmalade." Then he pulled his blankets back over his head and disappeared beneath them.

33

The special days we'd come here for had now arrived. There were lots of things about Beltane I still didn't know, and a lot of questions buzzed about inside my head. I guessed that Brother Adelard, the intellectual amongst the monks, might be able to provide me with some answers. Maybe the Irishman Liam could as well. But I suspected that Brother Fergus, the monk who was most expert on Celtic mythology, was an even better bet. I would see if I couldn't track the fellow down and engage him in conversation.

I took my time wandering about the island on this post-storm day. Signs of last night's storm were everywhere. The farmers were busy in their fields taking stock of the damage to their young crops and tidying up debris. It looked like their sheep had weathered the storm well, though, which I knew would be a huge relief to these hardy islanders. They didn't put all their eggs in one basket, but their sheep were one of their most important eggs.

I meandered along the edge of the island's eastern coast for a bit. The cove where the professor and I had visited the seal colony yesterday was deserted. But then, looking out to sea, I could just make out the small dark heads of the seals as they popped up and then disappeared one by one in a random fashion. They looked like they were enjoying themselves disporting in the water, but I suspected they were feeding. I stood and watched them for a few minutes, wishing I were a selkie and could join them in their frolics.

As I wandered, I thought about my five companions and why each of us "pilgrims" had come to this remote Welsh island. We had our reasons, and they weren't all the same. Wilkins, I felt sure, had come seeking some emotional release, in the hope of achieving some kind of personal atonement or solace. The Reverend Mason had come to provide support to Wilkins and to seek answers to spiritual questions of his own. Dr. Atkinson was here in the spirit of scientific inquiry. He wanted to know more about the possible existence of "ghosts," or what he called spiritual emanations. My father-in-law, Professor Challenger, was here in the spirit of scientific skepticism; he wanted to debunk what he considered to be the far-fetched notions of the others. Lord John Roxton was here for the sheer adventure of it. As for me, I'd originally come just to get a newspaper story. Now my motives seemed to be veering in a different direction, one I hadn't entirely sorted out just yet. Some self-imposed penance seemed to be involved, but penance for what I didn't know.

The monks didn't come together for their noontime meal in the refectory, but I made my way to the monastery anyway in hopes of locating Brother Fergus. I hoped to find him alone, if possible, since I thought that his answers to my questions might be more constrained in the presence of others. He seemed to me to be more philosophically sympathetic to the ancient Celtic mysteries, whereas his colleagues—especially Brothers Adelard, Anthony, and Thomas—were likely to be hostile to them.

When I got there I wandered about the old monastic site keeping a sharp eye out for Brother Fergus. I searched fruitlessly for a quarter of an hour, not finding him or any of the others. The place seemed strangely deserted. I went up to the terraced area where they'd been preparing their garden, but no luck there, either.

I was standing in the shade of the medieval tower, wondering where else I could look to find the bloke, when I heard the sound of footsteps slowly approaching from around the side of the ancient structure. Then the figure of a small man came into view. He stopped, startled, and stood there staring at me his eyes wide.

It was Brother Malachi. He stood there silently wringing his hands and staring at me with his huge greenish-brown eyes. Then to my surprise he began speaking to me.

"Emm . . . she be lookin' for you," he said in a strange, whispery voice. It was just about the first time I'd heard him say anything more than "amen" or "big storm."

"I'm sorry, *what*?" I replied.

He looked away from me and twisted the toes of one foot into the ground in front of him. "Emm, she be lookin' for you," he said again.

"*She*? Who is she, Brother Malachi? And how do you know this?"

"Em . . . a woman, sir," he said. "She says she's needin' to find you."

"A woman needs to find me?" I said, taken back. "*What* woman?"

"Em . . . don't rightly know, sir. Emm, . . , I think she's a spirit woman."

"A *spirit* woman," I gasped. What's a spirit woman? Where did you see this, uh, spirit woman, Brother Malachi?"

". . . well, sir . . . I didn't really see her. It was inside my head where I saw her, just inside my head."

I expelled a deep breath. "You see people inside your head?"

"Em . . . , sometimes I do, yes."

"What did this spirit woman say to you, Malachi?"

He raised his eyes to mine and paused for a moment while he stared straight into my face. "Emm . . . she asked me where you were. Said she been lookin' for you. Said she missed you. Said she needed to see you and tell you she was fine."

"Any idea who she was, Malachi? Did she tell you that?"

Brother Malachi shook his head. "Nuh uh," he whispered.

"Malachi, any idea how I might be able to find this spirit woman?"

He gave a shrug of his shoulders. "Can't say for certain. But spirits sometimes have a knack of appearing on Beltane and Samhain. Leastwise to me they do. Look round inside your head, maybe you'll find her in there. 'Bout the only advice I can give you."

I reached out and placed my hand on his upper arm. "Brother Malachi, thank you for bringing me this message. If she comes to you again, please tell her I'd like it very much if she could appear inside *my* head."

He nodded. I had a sense that speaking so many words had been hard for him. He shot me a quick flicker of a smile, then turned on his heel and scuttled away.

I stood alone in a quandary having no idea what to make of him or his message. *What in the hell?* I thought. *What in the hell?*

An hour later I finally succeeded in tracking down Brother Fergus. I found him in a small rocky cove a couple of hundred yards below the monastery. He was busy loading an old, wheeled cart with a pile of seaweed he'd amassed. He looked up as I approached.

"What are you doing?" I asked.

"Fertilizing the garden o' course."

"With seaweed?"

"And bird droppings."

"I'm a city lad. I had no idea."

"I guess you and your chums are learning lots of new things out here on the holy sland, eh?" he said. "Guess that's one of the reasons you came. Learn a few new things, have a few new experiences."

"Speaking of which," I said, "I'd like to ask you several things I've been wondering about."

"Of course. Fire away, my friend."

"The Isle of Avalon. You familiar with it?"

As he was collecting his various bits—rake, gardening gloves, towel or wiping his sweaty bow—he said "Isle of Avalon? Oh yeah, I've heard of it. Never been to the legendary place, though." He chuckled softly.

"So, this island isn't it?"

"Not so far as I know. Do you know where that name comes from?"

"Insulas Avalonia?" I replied.

"The Isle of Apples. Quite right. And once this island probably did have quite a large grove of apple trees. A lot more than just that one brave tree that stands there today. Those old monks must've had themselves a flourishing grove of them, trees that yielded a crop ample enough to supply 'em with barrels of cider. The Bardsey apple tree is probably the sole descendant of that ancient apple grove. But I don't think this isle was ever 'the Fruitful Isle' the old books talk about. This harsh old place is far too inhospitable. It's rather a miracle that the one tree has managed to survive."

"Tell me about Avalon, if you would?" Together we began pushing the heavily loaded cart slowly up the narrow trail. Working in tandem, it wasn't too hard going, but he would have had a much tougher time of it if I hadn't turned up to lend a hand.

"Supposedly, Avalon is where Caliburn—or Excalibur—King Arthur's famous sword, was forged. And it was to Avalon that King Arthur was taken after the last battle by Morgan le Fay to have his wounds tended to. Some works say Morgan ruled there over the Ladies of Avalon, her eight sisters, each of whom possessed a special mastery—of music, astronomy, and so on."

"Sounds rather like the Nine Muses of classical mthology," I said.

"Lots of commonalities amongst the ancient myths and legends," he replied. "Morgan, Arthur's half-sister, was reputed to be gifted in the healing arts. The island itself bore all kinds of fruit, not just apples, and it needed no tending. They had no need to be hauling any seaweed up to the garden terrace to enrich the soil as we are doing, more proof that Ynys Enlli isn't Avalon. Let's us stop for a moment and have a breather. Need to mop my brow."

"Beltane," I said, as we stood there catching our breaths.

"What's so special about the first day of May? Why was it considered a major holy day?"

"First day of the summer half of the year. Kind of like New Year's Day for the ancient Celts. A day of fresh beginnings and a renewal of the cycle of life. Like the blossoms you saw on the apple tree, signifying a new start."

"Is it a time when it's possible for mortals to come in contact with the faerie realm?" I asked. "I read that in a book in a London library."

A stern look crept over his face and he looked me straight in the eye. "That something you want to do?" he said seriously. "Come in contact with the faerie realm?"

"Don't know. Maybe."

"A dangerous business," he said after a long pause. "You'd best take care. Not so long ago some mortals responded to the calls of the Fair Folk. Those foolish mortals were never seen again."

"Seriously?"

He gave a one-shouldered shrug. "That's what they say. It was before my time on the island."

"How would I find the faerie realm if I wished to do that?" I asked.

"No, my friend, you don't wish to do that. Stay away from those old faerie places, especially tonight, tomorrow, and the next day. Stay away from the faerie places and leave the Fair Folk be. Safest advice I can give ya."

"The faerie places? I haven't seen anywhere on the island

that looks like a faerie place."

"Oh, there's at least a couple o' them. You've seen the apple tree, eh? That be one o' them. But the truly dangerous one's the old faerie mound."

"I haven't seen any faerie mounds. Tell me where it is so I can be sure to avoid it."

Fergus gave me the bent-eye, then clammed up on me. I could tell he was reluctant to say much more on the matter.

"The farmers know enough to avoid it, too," he said at last. "They plow around it and leave it be. So you should leave it be as well. They do look innocent enough, them old faerie folk. Don't trust your eyes. They ain't evil, exactly, but they certainly ain't as harmless as they look, neither. Not by a long chalk." I nodded my understanding.

I tucked away Fergus's information and advice. I knew it was good advice. Still, the possible existence of the spirit woman whom Brother Malachi had told me about served as a lure to me. If she didn't find me, then maybe I could find her. Maybe I could find her at one of the faerie sites, on Beltane Eve. That is, if I dared to risk it.

34

We trooped single file up the trail toward the monastic complex to join the monks for their evening meal, each of us lost in our own thoughts. Tonight, I planned to switch things up and not sit straight across from Brother Malachi, to demonstrate to my compatriots that the young monk was not fixated on me. Besides, the things he said earlier in the day had made me more than a little bit anxious. I'd tried to shrug them off as the thoughts of a slightly deranged mind. Still, I hadn't forgotten that we were on the verge of Beltane, allegedly a time when things beyond the realm of the normal are said to occur.

I waited outside the door to the refectory until all of my companions had gone in. Then I did as well and snagged the seat on the end of the bench nearest the door. The monks hadn't come in yet, but I assumed that when they did, being creatures of habit, they would occupy their regular seats. I was wrong. Malachi entered last and plopped himself down on the end of the bench right across from me. His eyes glanced up at me. There was a half-grin on his lips.

Brother Anthony, tonight's cook, carried in a huge pot of soup. An oniony fragrance filled the room. As he ladled the soup into the bowls, I could see that it was chock full of potatoes, carrots, and bits of lamb along with a plentitude of onions. As usual, the soup was powerfully spiced—salt, black pepper, thyme, rosemary, sage, and surely some others. The breadbaskets circulated, the cider and apple juice were poured, and grace was said, followed by a loud chorus of "amens."

Conversation mostly concerned the storm. Liam reminisced about a great storm he once experienced in the west of Ireland. Brother Adelard held forth for a few minutes about a great storm described in a sixth-century work of annals. Brother Anthony recalled the first great storm he'd lived through on the island, his very first year as a monk here. Our group had little to add.

Malachi, as usual, remained entirely mute. He clearly liked the thick, savory soup, which he soaked up with thick chunks of bread. After draining his tankard of cider, he filled it again but didn't drink. He looked across at me, grinned, then he nudged the tankard across the table. He made a slight dip of his head toward me. Giving me a meaningful stare with his huge green-brown eyes, he was urging me to drink.

I thought about the strange, self-imposed abstinence I'd been following for the past week. I wasn't sure what had brought that about. But the truth was, I had found it curiously satisfying. Maybe, now that we had completed our pilgrimage and were on the very cusp of Beltane, maybe now it was time for me to end my abstemious ways and revert to my normal habits. That seemed to be what Malachi was suggesting in shoving the tankard toward me. Did he know something that I didn't?

I realized that Professor Challenger was looking at me. So was Malachi. So were my companions. So were the other monks.

I wrapped my fingers around the tankard and slowly raised it to my lips. "Yaki dah," I said. Then I drank deeply. The potent cider tasted sweet and tangy.

There was silence in the refectory. After several beats I heard Liam say, "Oh, yeah, he's an Irishman."

The scrumpy hit me hard. It was even stronger than I had expected. Since I'd gone quite a few days without alcohol, I knew I'd best go easy on it from here on out. If I didn't, I'd soon be under the table.

"Yaki dah," the professor said, looking at me.

I glanced across at Brother Malachi. He was beaming me a wide toothy grin. Then I saw his lips moving. Silently his lips said, "She will find you. Tonight."

I stared at him, not knowing if he'd actually just said what I thought he'd said; or if it was the scrumpy-jack that had taken hold of me. I knew that the alcohol was already giving me a bit of a warm buzz.

35

After the meal, *McCauley Wilkins and the Reverend Mason once again joined the monks for their evening service. Their pilgrim compatriots headed back to the hostel, except for Ted Malone, who had wandered off somewhere by himself. He'd been doing quite a bit of that lately.*

Strangely, only three of the seven monks attended the service. Absent were Brothers Liam, Fergus, Thomas, and Malachi.

"Where are the others?" McCauley whispered to the reverend.

"Don't know," came his whispered reply.

"I guess we are it," declared Brother Anthony, glancing at the empty seats. He seemed slightly offended by the absence of the others.

"It's May Day Eve," Brother Adelard reminded him in a low voice.

"Ah, that must be it. Maybe I should change my topic and speak of the Righteous Pagans." His comment caused Adelard

and Aled to smile politely.

McCauley glanced at the reverend, who whispered, "I'll explain that to you later." McCauley nodded.

"What I will address," Brother Anthony went on, "are the implications of verses 1 to 6 of Psalm 90." He proceeded to read the verses aloud, ending with the admonition to beware "the noon-day demon." The words of the psalm brought a chill to McCauley Wilkins because they reminded him of the little stone demon he'd been so entranced by at Chester Cathedral. As a result, Wilkins's thoughts wandered freely for the next several minutes and he paid scant attention to the monk's learned disquisition. Before he knew it, the monks were singing their closing hymn and the service was concluded.

As the two *of them walked together back to the hostel, the reverend explained to McCauley Wilkins the conundrum of the Righteous Pagan, the good person who had the misfortune to live before Christ and so couldn't be a Christian, which meant that such a person was excluded from eternal salvation.*

"Doesn't seem fair," McCauley said.

"No, but that's often true in this life of ours."

"Do you think he was implying that the absent monks were pagans?"

"Probably. And that their absence was likely connected to tonight being the eve of a major pagan holy day."

"Beltane is May Day?"

"Oh, yes. Much revered by the Celts."

"So, the others were off celebrating a pagan holy day?"

"Possibly they were. But my guess would be more that they felt a bit betwixt and between, and thus not entirely comfortable at a Christian service on the night of a major non-Chrisitan celebration, one that was an important part of their Celtic heritage."

"I can see that," McCauley said, with a shoulder shrug.

When they reached the hostel, McCauley Wilkins didn't go in. He told the reverend he wanted to walk a bit more on his own before retiring for the evening.

"The professor said he was willing to share his Talisker with us tonight to celebrate May Day Eve," the Reverend Mason said, with raised eyebrows. "That's not an invitation you often get."

"Maybe I'll be back in time to join in," Wilkins said.

36

After the meal, three of my companions—my father-in-law, Lord Roxton, and Dr. Atkinson—returned to the hostel. McCauley Wilkins and the Reverend Mason once again joined the monks for their evening service. I decided to remain behind for a while poking about in the general area of the monastic complex. I intended to get free of my companions and spend Beltane Eve entirely on my own.

I was drawn to the little graveyard that lay close beside the monastic complex, a small area I hadn't paid much attention to earlier. Now, for some reason, it had a pull on me. Anyway, it was a way to kill some time before doing what I really wanted to do, which was slip down to the farm fields and see if I couldn't track down the faerie mound Brother Fergus had told me about, the faerie mound he'd advised me to steer clear of.

The tidy little burial ground appeared to be the private graveyard they'd used exclusively for the deceased monks.

As I studied the dates on the gravestones, I saw that they extended as far back as the eighteenth century. The grass-covered grave mounds had been laid out in neat rows, and at the head of each mound rose a simple grave marker. Most of the graves were marked by stone crosses, the names and dates having been incised into the stone. A few of the markers were in the style of Celtic crosses, while surprisingly a few others bore entirely different emblems, some non-Christian. On one I saw a Star of David and incised into another one was a crescent moon and star.

Suddenly, out of the corner of my eye, I sensed movement above me on the trail that led up to the terraced garden. It was Brother Thomas. He was apparently skipping out on the church service; probably excusing himself so he could check on his newly emerging plants. He didn't seem to notice me down below watching him.

When I directed my attention back to the gravestones, I sensed additional movement. As I stood before a grave marked by a moss-covered Celtic cross, I realized that a small white furry face was staring at me from around the bottom the shaft. It was the face of a cat.

"Hello, Pud," I said. The cat was shy, but after looking me over good, she deigned to move cautiously out from behind the grave marker. Apparently I'd passed muster with her.

"You're a lovely creature," I said, reaching down to pet her, which to my surprise she allowed me to do. "Is this your private domain? Or have you wandered up from one of the farms?"

"Gwynnie," someone called out.

"Guess your name isn't Pud," I said softly.

"Oh, there you are." It was Brother Malachi, slightly out of breath.

When he saw me, he said, "Makin' friends with me cat, hmm? She does be a sweet one but also a sly one." The normally taciturn Malachi seemed to have become downright talkative of late. It was almost as if *my* drinking of his cider had loosened *his* tongue.

"Her name is Gwyn?"

"Ya didn't think I'd go so far as to call her Blackie, did ya?" he said with his customary grin.

"She looks pure as the driven snow," I said.

"Hah!" he scoffed. "She ain't, I can tell ya."

Malachi scooped up the cat, and she began purring and rubbing the side of her face against his.

"She likes you," I said.

"She's just buttering me up. Wants me ta feed her."

"Which I'm guessing you are about to do."

"Oh, yes." Brother Malachi pulled a folded cloth from his pocket and placed it on the ground beside the grave mound. The cat leapt from his clutches and attacked the food inside the cloth. I guessed it was bits of fish.

"No church service for you tonight?"

"Nuh uh. Not on Beltane. Wouldn't be right. So, you be studyin' the old grave markers, eh?" he asked.

"Mostly just looking at the names and dates." I glanced at the inscription on the one where I first saw the cat. The marker atop the grave was a small Celtic cross and the name on it was "Fintan."

"Fintan," I said, reading the name out loud. "Name rings a bell with me. Now, I wonder where I've come across that name before?" Then I remembered that I'd encountered it in my reading in Dr. Williams' library in London. Fintan was an important figure out of early Celtic mythology, a fellow who'd actually survived Noah's Flood, first in the form of a salmon, and then down through the ages in a succession of physical forms—eagle, stag, etc., and finally, once again, as a man.

"Say, Malachi, your cat wouldn't be Fintan the White, would she?"

"Eh, what?"

"You know, the transmigration of the soul? Fintan was really good at that, his soul moving from creature to creature every few hundred years or so. Maybe Gwynnie is Fintan?"

"And maybe you drank a bit too much o' that potent cider, eh?" He had a point.

"Say, Malachi, that old faerie mound Fergus was telling me about, where exactly is it?"

"Fergus was tellin' ya about it? Then I suppose it's all right for me to also. It be easy ta find, just a couple hundred yards beyond the farmer's byre." Then Malachi, wondering if maybe he'd said more than he should have, scrunched up his face and gave me a squinty-eyed look. "But ya don't want ta be a-going there tonight, oh no ya don't. Not tonight, not on Beltane Eve. Not *never* on Beltane Eve." He looked at me nervously.

"Come on, Gwynnie," he said, scooping up the cat. He seemed eager to end the conversation.

I glanced once more at the name Fintan inscribed on the gravestone. And when I looked up again, both Malachi and his white cat had disappeared.

Dark was falling fast as I made my way down to the low-lying agricultural area of the island. No one seemed to be about. Farmers keep different hours than city-folks—early to bed, early to rise. I didn't know what hours faerie folk kept, but I assumed that tonight it probably involved midnight, which was still several hours away.

Malachi had said the faerie mound was only a short distance beyond a byre. I didn't know what a byre was, but I reckoned it shouldn't be too hard to locate the faerie mound, if the farmers plowed around it and gave it a wide berth, as Fergus had said.

I meandered for a bit before finally finding the area I was looking for. I passed a small outbuilding or shed, which I assumed might well be the byre. And then there, not a great distance before me, was the faerie mound. It was a small rounded grassy hillock encircled by a ring of low stones. From where I stood I could see that there was a darker section in one side of the little hill; I guessed it might be a kind of entranceway into the mound. Like the farmers, I planned to give the little hill a wide berth.

I looked about for somewhere to take up my station while I kept watch on the faerie mound. I intended to observe—from a safe distance—whatever Beltane Eve activities might occur there tonight. Maybe seventy or eighty yards from the mound I spotted a pair of standing stones. That seemed like a safe place to lurk, I crouched down low to the ground and leaned my back against one of them. That way, I hoped, I would be able to observe any festivities about the mound without anyone paying any attention to me.

The night sky was thick with stars, the distant sea sounds muted, the farmland surrounding me eerily silent. The air was fresh and cool, but not what you would call chilly. The grassy turf formed a soft cushion beneath me, but the upright stone I leaned against was cold and hard against my back. Despite that, I closed my eyes and managed to doze off, knowing it was still a couple of hours until midnight.

When I awoke, it took me a moment to get my bearings. I quickly realized that I wasn't in the pilgrims' hostel. No, I'd been sprawled out asleep against some ancient stone, all alone in a farmer's field on a tiny island off the northwest coast of Wales. What did I think I was doing?

As my brain slowly cleared, all of my senses started to

come alive. I smelled the odors of animals in nearby pens, heard the rustlings of small creatures in clumps of furze and heather, and now I saw the shape of the faerie mound less than a hundred yards away more distinctly than before. And then suddenly I had a premonition that I was not as alone as I thought. Something was about to happen here, and I had no idea what. I felt a frisson, more of excitement than fear, though fear wasn't entirely absent either, and the hairs on the back of my neck had begun to prickle.

Then, as if from a great distance, I began to hear music. First the soft rhythmic beating of drums, then above the drums the high, almost shrill, sound of flutes or tin whistles. The eerie music seemed to be coming from inside the mound. Then a bright light shined forth from the entranceway to the mound. Human shapes began emerging from the mound. They were the shapes of the beings playing the musical instruments I'd been hearing. The musicians filed forth, then stood flanking the mound's entrance as a multitude of others slowly emerged. They were normal-sized men, women, and children, all of them resplendent in their beauty, and all of them were singing. Their high, mellifluent voices blended together in some exotic melody. It was like nothing I had ever heard before. Their music was entrancing. It was almost as if they were putting a spell on me. I felt excitement only slightly tinged with fear.

A tall dark man stepped forth from the mound and then behind him came a fair, shining woman in a radiant green dress, her long golden tresses falling to her waist. Adorning her head I saw a golden circlet into which was set a red stone that glowed like a burning flame. Behind them a great many more figures similarly attired began to emerge from the mound. Each one wore a gold circlet about their head, each of which bore a brightly shining red gemstone They filed out and formed into a procession, and then these comely, luminous beings began moving in a wide circle about the mound. The whole scene filled me with wonderment. Were these the "Fair Folk" I had read about?

A radiance emanated from the opening in the mound, but a glow also shone forth from the track the procession followed. For these dancing, singing beings themselves possessed a curious luminosity; a greenish effulgence seemed to radiate from each of them. Their faces shone with the vitality of youth, and as they proceeded, they sang and laughed gleefully. The nearer to me they came, these blithe spirits, the more the light they radiated increased. They looked lovely and ecstatically happy. Their carefree exuberance was infectious, and I felt myself being drawn to them. I found myself longing to join the joyful throng. I wanted to be one of them, wanted to add my voice to theirs in their exotic melody. I felt totally enraptured by them and their carefree existence.

One of them, a young woman in a green, diaphanous gown, stepped forth from the procession and stood for a moment looking at me. She was as beautiful as a dream, and her gleaming eyes seemed to reflect the moonlight. She raised her arms and gestured towards me. She was inviting me to join them. With all my being I wanted to do that, wanted to go with her to whatever world she lived in, a world where, I suspected, ordinary time and space held no sway.

I had begun rising to my feet to go to her when I felt the soft, gentle touch of a hand on my shoulder. Then I heard a soft voice say, "No, stay. She's not the one." I knew the touch of that hand. I knew the soft voice. I wanted so desperately to go. But the voice told me not to. So did the hand that gently lay upon my shoulder.

The young woman in the green gown stood before me, extending her arms toward me, a golden circlet with a glowing red stone atop it held in her hands. Her eyes and her face implored me to take the gift she was offering and to come with her and join the throng. I felt the tug of her will upon me. I took one step forward, then stopped. Fergus had warned me. Malachi had warned me. And now the person I had loved more than any other in my life had told me to "stay."

I looked at the young woman who still awaited my decision. Then, sadly, I shook my head. Her face bore a sorrowful look. The golden circlet dropped from her hands and the red gemstone disappeared from view in the tall grass before her. The young woman turned slowly about and re-joined the procession. In a trice I lost sight of her amongst all the other revelers. A profound melancholy came upon me, a profound sense of loss.

For another short while the Fair Folk continued their frolics, but then at last they began trooping back into the mound from whence they had come. The luminosity of their presence faded slowly away. Finally, so did the strains of their music. They were gone.

The night settled back to what it had been before. But that wasn't the case for me.

37

McCauley Wilkins *had no intention of joining the others at the pilgrims' hostel for a nip of Talisker. For reasons he didn't understand, it was his desire to spend May Eve not in the company of his companions but in that of just the old apple tree. He had come to think of the tree as a living being, one that intrigued him and comforted him. While he knew it wasn't a sentient being, he rejoiced in the tree's strength and resilience. Even having been shorn of its lovely white blossoms by the recent storm, it still possessed a strange beauty for McCauley; in fact, it possessed a powerful, almost magnetic, pull that drew him to it.*

It was dark now, but his eyes had adjusted, and he easily found the barn which partially shielded the tree from the harsh western winds. A gibbous moon would be up in another hour or two, but for now the night sky was bejeweled with a myriad of stars, the like of which he'd never seen in the city. He knew little of the constellations, but he could readily pick out Venus, "the evening star," and Mars, the "angry red planet," and in the northern sky, the Big Dipper.

As he stood behind the barn, he took in the dark form of the old tree, its branches contorted into twisted shapes and strange configurations. He supposed that to the eyes of many people the tree would appear ugly and misshapen; to him, that was not at all the case. McCauley Wilkins imagined commissioning a London artist to create a metal sculpture for him, one that captured the tree's harsh beauty. For now, however, he was content to gaze upon the Bardsey Apple Tree in actuality.

He and his companions would be leaving the island in another day or two, and it was highly unlikely that he would ever be in this place again. He had no way to preserve its memory other than to drink it in deeply now and let his mind and body register and absorb these precious moments.

He lowered himself down behind the barn and leaned back against its weathered wooden siding. He didn't find it at all disconcerting to be sitting there alone in the dark. He had the tree and the stars as his companions. They wouldn't make snide remarks at his expense, as Professor Challenger and Lord Roxton were wont to do. He excluded Ted Malone from that group because he'd begun to feel a curious kinship with the young newspaper man, over and above the fact that he owed Malone a huge debt of gratitude for saving his life.

Still, at the moment, he was glad that Ted was elsewhere, where exactly he had no idea, but fortunately not here. For now, he desired nothing more than to be here alone with the tree.

Dark night enveloped him. This was the most relaxed he'd felt since leaving London, actually the most relaxed he'd felt since he'd received the shocking news of his wife's death. He breathed out a soft sigh and leaned back against the barn's solid wall. He looked upward and drank in the sight of the myriad stars once more. Then his eyelids began to droop, and he slid slowly into a half-slumber. He found himself entering a trance-like state, one that hovered between consciousness and unconsciousness. He could still feel the solid wall behind him and see the dark shape of the tree before him. But what he was about to witness in his half-conscious state bore little resemblance to real life as he had always known it.

The apple tree *swayed gently in the sea breeze. McCauley ran his eyes over it, beginning with the bits of roots that showed above ground, then up the tree's slender central trunk to the main branches and then its lesser limbs. As he looked at it, he imagined it as a human being, as the sensuous body of a woman. Then, to his astonishment, as he watched the old tree, he saw it begin to undergo a slow and subtle transformation. Gradually it was taking on a human form,* *the form indeed of a beautiful, desirable woman.*

How could this be? Was he inebriated? He knew he should be frightened by the bizarre sight he was witnessing and yet he wasn't. He was enthralled. The tree had gradually transmogrified into the figure of a perfectly shaped woman, though a woman of extraordinary size. Her diaphanous gown did little to conceal her splendid physical form, indeed, it accentuated it. As McCauley stared at her he realized that the tree-woman looked familiar to him. Now, too, he caught the hint of a familiar fragrance, not of apples but of roses, Yardley's English Roses. To his astonishment, the tree had become a larger-than-life replication of Felicity, his late wife.

The tree-woman leaned toward McCauley and her familiar face, reflecting the now-risen moon, shone down upon him. She extended her limbs toward him but didn't touch him. Then she addressed him, speaking in a firm and intense voice, though not with anger.

"Now we are together, as we have been before," she said. "It is the 'before' that we must cherish, not the more recent times." Then she began speaking to him of times long past, presenting him with a vista of remembrance.

"Do you recall the sweet opening of our love? Do the memories of our first meetings still reside in your heart? They do in mine. How could we have let them languish and die? I will forgive you, if you will forgive me.

"Do you remember that summer afternoon in Cambridge when we strolled along the Granta, eventually making our way to Grantchester? We sat beneath the trees in the orchard delighting in each other's presence. We were together as one, spiritually and physically."

McCauley sat there speechlessly in his trance-like state listening to the recitation of his late wife as she chronicled their life together: first rehearsing their many early happy moments, then passing on to later times when the magic had begun to fade away. Then her words became more rueful. She spoke with regret of their growing estrangement, taking the onus for that largely upon herself—to a greater extent than McCauley believed was fair.

"You didn't cause my death," she firmly declared. "I myself was the causer of it. I wanted to put the blame on you, torment you with a sense of your guilt; but I knew that hadn't really been true. Oh, yes, you have your frailties and imperfections like any other person; but you did your best as it pertains to me and to our relationship. I failed to reciprocate. McCauley, you must go on now and live a full life, a fulfilled life. You must do that, dear husband, you must do that." Her eyes stared into his.

Was she trying to expiate her own sense of guilt? That possibility crossed McCauley's mind. In any case, her words served to expiate his sense of guilt.

With a wan smile, she reached down toward him—

still in his trance-like state—and touched him for the first time, pressing the four fingers of one hand firmly against his brow. He sensed a stirring inside his head, then just for a brief moment a sharp pain. It felt to him as if she was removing something from inside his body, from inside his brain. It seemed to him she was extracting some object from his physical person. For just a fraction of a second the carved-stone figure at Chester Cathedral, the little imp that had so intrigued him, flashed through his mind. He remembered the night when he'd imagined the little demon detaching itself from the cathedral wall, coming to him and becoming absorbed into him. Had he been serving as host for the devilish little creature for the last several days? Had the evil being somehow manifested itself within him for some demonic purpose? Had the tree-woman now put paid to the malicious little imp and his machinations?

The tree-woman withdrew her hand and then her arm away from McCauley. Her entire body pulled back. Her eyes sparkled and her sad smile flitted again for just a moment on her lips. Slowly, her physical form began shifting. Her female body was dematerializing and turning back into the form of the apple tree. Felicity was gone, and McCauley Wilkins knew in his heart that he would never see her again.

Some indeterminate *time later—the moon had dipped low into the west and dawn was creeping up in the east—Wilkins* *emerged from his trance-like state. He discovered that now he was not alone, for a pair of men sat beside him, one snugged up against each of his shoulders. The men were Professor George Edward Challenger and the London journalist, Ted Malone.*

38

I wasn't sure how I came to be there sitting near the apple tree in the company of McCauley Wilkins and my father-in-law. I had no recollection of my actions since being left forlorn and abandoned at the fairy mound.

I still felt a profound sadness at not joining the procession and going off with the Fair Folk into their mysterious world. I felt that I had been offered the chance of a lifetime and I had declined—though not entirely of my own volition. Why had I declined? Partly, perhaps, because of the cautionary warnings I'd received from the monks Fergus and Malachi. But most especially because Enid, my dearly departed and much beloved wife, had advised me to. And maybe also because I knew in my innermost being that it would be a colossal mistake, one that would put my immortal soul at risk.

But, oh, how I had wanted to go with the Fair Folk and the woman who'd beckoned to me. And now, reminded of the words of John Keats, I sat there alone "pale and loitering," where the sedge had withered on the lake and no birds sang. Would a sense of desolation hover over me for the rest of my life? Of course, it was far too soon to say. I couldn't help giving an audible groan.

"Ted," Professor Challenger said, "was that you, my lad? You sound a bit downcast. Unlike Mac here, you seem to have had a rough night of it. Are you, perhaps, in need of the hair of the dog?"

"Ugh," I said. "No more potent cider ever again for me."

"What you need, my lad, is a couple rashers of bacon and a plate of scrambled eggs."

"Appeals to me," Wilkins said, cheerfully. "I am ravenous. Let's go eat."

When we reached the hostel, we discovered that our compatriots were still in the arms of sleep. But not for long, for my father-in-law immediately began to bellow:

" *'Get up! Get up for shame! The blooming morn*
   Upon her wings presents the god unshorn.
   Get up, sweet slugs-a-bed and see
   The dew bespangling herb and tree.' "

Three startled heads poked out from beneath bedcovers. There was a long moment of shocked silence until Lord John Roxton responded by shouting, "Bloody *Herrick?* Not bloody Herrick! Couldn't you at least have made it Donne or Milton?"

"Did they write any May Day poems?"

"Of course they didn't. Thy weren't bloody pagans like Herrick. Totally civilized Christian chaps. And where the devil is my bloody morning tea, anyway?"

"It's on its way, Lord John, so relax and imagine yourself out there a-Maying with Herrick's Corinna. Just give us half a mo', eh?"

After managing to get down a few mouthfuls of breakfast and two cups of tea—no hair of the dog for me—I climbed into my bunk and pulled the covers over my head. I awoke alone in the hostel about mid-afternoon. I'd no idea what the others were up to, though I felt confident they hadn't gone a-Maying.

By the time I'd fully roused myself, there was still no one else about. Hoping to have a quiet word with my father-in-law out of earshot of the others, I set off in search of him. It was down at the seal cove where I found him, as I expected, bidding adieu to his sleek-coated friends. His delight in these creatures amused me. This time Challenger wasn't singing to them, they were singing to him—although calling it singing was giving them the benefit of the doubt.

"These gentle fellas," the professor said, gesturing toward the barking seals, do you think they spent May Eve a-whoopin' it up? Took on their human forms and frolicked with the Fairy Folk the way some of the rest of us did?"

"Some of the rest of us? Were you in on the frolicking yourself, sir?"

"Only after my fashion, Ted. Not to the same extent as some of you young sparks."

"I didn't frolic, sir. I was no more than a passive observer."

"Is that so?" He gave me a meaningful look. Had he been keeping an eye on me? No, surely not. In any case I hadn't *done* anything to be ashamed of, at least not quite.

"Sir, so you frolicked after your fashion? Care to elaborate?"

"Spirit Folk," he grumped. "The fact is, I had a curious encounter with one of those creatures last night, Ted. As least, I think I did, unless it was all in my imagination."

"An encounter? What sort of encounter?"

"You remember that funny business the other night when our whole group dreamed of succubae? This time around the succubus who appeared to me had the audacity to turn up into the form of my dear, dear Jessie."

"My word, sir. And what happened?"

"Just toying with me, she was, though toying may not be the right word. No, Ted, she was trying to entice me, debauch me, trying to lure me into putting my immortal soul at risk."

I gave my father-in-law a wide-eyed stare.

"You're aware of the old belief that when two people kiss they exchange souls, correct? So, if you kiss a spirit-being, then you've taken in their soul and they now possess yours."

"Like Dr. Faustus and the spirit of Helen of Troy that he conjured up?"

"That's it, Ted, just like in Marlowe's play. But in this

case the baggage made a crucial error. Just as we were about to kiss she spoke the wrong words."

"What wrong words did she speak?"

"Actually, it wasn't what she said, it was what she didn't say. She didn't say, "A gift, my beloved." Jessica always said that as a prelude to a kiss, she never once failed to do it. I never knew if she meant she was giving a gift to me or she was receiving one from me. Either way, it was a lover's gift."

"So when the succubus didn't say those words, you rebuffed her?" He nodded. "And then what happened?" I asked.

"Don't know. The next thing I knew, I was sitting there alongside you and Wilkins near the apple tree. No idea how I got there."

"So at least she didn't walk away with your immortal soul."

"Far as I know, I still possess the blessed thing."

"I hope that goes for both of us, sir."

"You, too, eh?"

"Sadly, yes. I didn't have quite the same experience as you, but a little along those lines."

"But you managed to preserve your integrity."

"Yes, . . . I guess so, but I needed some assistance to do it."

"Then all's well that ends well."

39

On our last night on the island we planned to eat a final meal with the monks and then, out of gratitude and respect, all of us would attend their post-meal church service, even Challenger and Lord Roxton. The boatman, Brother Anthony told us, would be arriving at mid-morning tomorrow to take us back to Aberdaron. So, this would be our final opportunity to spend time with the monks.

Both groups of men had taken their customary seats on the benches in the refectory. This time I had positioned myself in the very middle of my companions and, predictably, Brother Malachi had seated himself straight across from me.

Soon the familiar rituals were set in motion—the saying of grace, the chorus of "amens" and the passing of the plates to the end of the table. There was little conversation until Professor Challenger, as was his wont, introduced a contentious topic.

"Almost all of the important Christian Holy Days," he

declared, "occur in close proximity to ancient, pre-Christian holy days: All Saints Day was superimposed upon Samain; Lammas paired with Lughnasa; Candlemas with Imbolg; St. John's Day with the summer solstice and Michaelmas with the fall equinox; and so on, even including Christmas and Easter. But there seems to be one major exception to the pattern: Beltane. There's no major Christian holy day right now, right here at the beginning of May. Why is that? I wonder. Why no holy day right now?"

I looked across at Brother Malachi whose face bore the blankest of looks. Unlike the others, he hadn't swiveled his head in the direction of Brother Adelard, the man the monks expected to speak for them. Had Malachi even been listening? The little jug-eared fellow seemed more abstracted than usual, more "fey," as my gran-mum would say.

"Ah," Adelard finally said, "why no Christian holiday at the beginning of May? Because there's really no need. May, and often early June, are already loaded up with holy days— Ascension Day, Pentecost, Whitsuntide, Trinity Sunday, the dates of which are dependent upon the date of Easter; they are all moveable feasts, as they say."

"Still," my father-in-law insisted, "it really does seem kind of odd that one of the major pagan holidays would remain unmatched—unchallenged, as it were—by Christianity."

Malachi *had* been listening, because his eyes suddenly sparkled and grew wide. Some of the other monks fidgeted a bit uncomfortably at Professor Challenger's borderline blasphemous words.

"Sir," Brother Adelard said, "we welcome all pilgrims to this holy island, and we respect each pilgrim's personal beliefs, even ones with which some of us may thoroughly disagree. If you find it strange that there's no major Christian holiday at the beginning of May, you are free to hold that view. I do not share it. The early Christian fathers obviously saw no need."

"I find," the Reverend Mason said, "that there's an implied Christian message of optimism and fresh exuberance in the old May Day rituals. I, too, see no need for there to be a specific Christian holy day to counteract such a message, since for once the messages are in concert with each other."

"And yet," Lord Roxton said, "perhaps there was some other reason why the early Christians choose not to superimpose one of their days on an important pagan day?"

"Yes?" shot back Brother Anthony. "Like what?"

"Maybe they decided it was wiser not to stir up certain ancient powers, ancient powers they decided were best left alone."

"Stuff and nonsense," Adelard said. "They knew full well that the Christian Saints and Angels are capable of taking on the most powerful of demonic forces. Didn't Saint Michael confront and vanquish Lucifer himself, consigning the fallen angel, now called Satan, to the fiery lake?"

"I don't doubt that, sir," Lord Roxton said. "I was merely suggesting a possible answer to the question posed by my friend, Professor Challenger."

"But why would there be any need to challenge so hopeful and benign a day as May Day?" the Reverend Mason said, reiterating his earlier comment. "It surely poses no threat to Christians and indeed underscores a basic Christian message."

At that the moment we all heard a soft chuckle from Brother Malachi. Then he said very softly but with an accompanying grin, "Benign." The reverend's word obviously had amused him.

After intentionally stirring things up, my father-in-law spent the next few minutes trying to mollify the monks. He expressed his great appreciation for their hospitality and intimated that we would be offering a substantial donation to their cause in support of others pilgrims who wished to visit the holy island. We knew that the alms provided by their pilgrim visitors constituted the monks' primary means of support, and that it was left up to their visitors to determine the size of their gifts. We (me being the one exception) were a particularly well-heeled group of visitors, so they might assume our largess would be substantial.

As the cheeseboard was circulating at the end of the meal, I looked up and saw Brother Malachi's eyes gazing at my face. Knowing he had my attention, his lips began to form words.

"Glad you didn't go," he whispered so low that I was reading his lips more than hearing his words. He was not grinning now. He was as sober-faced as I had ever seen him.

I formed words of my own which I whispered back at him: "You saved me. I will always be grateful."

He shook his head. "*She* saved you," he whispered.

I don't think anyone else at the table was aware of our exchange. Not unless it was my keen-witted, rascally father-in-law.

40

From the group of monks, only Brothers Anthony and Malachi came to see us off. Brother Anthony was as glib as usual. He expressed at some length his thanks to us for coming on our pilgrimage and for our generous donation. He hoped our visit had proved everything we had wanted it to be, perhaps subtly implying that he knew we hadn't come for reasons similar to those of most of their visiting pilgrims. He wished us a safe journey back to London and said he would be pleased if at some future time we might return to the holy island. He said that he and his fellow monks had found our visit most stimulating.

"So that you will not forget us," he said, "I have brought each of you a small token to commemorate your visit." He gestured to Malachi, who stepped forward. Brother Malachi proceeded to drape a leather lanyard around the neck of each of us. Attached to the lanyards were scallop shells.

"The shell," Brother Anthony said, "is the ancient symbol of pilgrimage. You are all pilgrims, and now I welcome each of you to the ancient fraternity of pilgrims."

Brother Malachi put the leather thong about my neck last of all, and immediately after he had, I felt him surreptitiously pressing a small cloth pouch into my hand. I guess he wanted me to have a special gift, perhaps a token of the connection each of us felt with the other. He was a kind, gentle fellow. I would miss him.

The little farewell ceremony completed, Brother Anthony shook hands with each of us. Brother Malachi stood there silently, a half-grin on his lips. Since he didn't attempt to shake anyone's hand, I stepped to him, reached out and gripped his.

"Guardian angels," I said in a low voice, causing his eyes to widen, "I've come around to believing in them." As he took in my words, his grin broadened to full face.

The hotel owner in Aberdaron, knowing that we were on our way, had managed to arrange transportation in a construction company's lorry. For a modest fee, the driver was willing to take us all the way to Bangor. The journey took the entire afternoon, and by the time we got there the light was fading fast.

"Well, shall we look in on the Baron and his brood?" Professor Challenger asked. "I think they are expecting us to."

"Wouldn't want to disappoint them," the Reverend Mason said. "And I certainly wouldn't mind sleeping in a proper bed for a change."

"Probably no succubae in Castle Penhenthy, though," came Lord Roxton's droll remark

"Thank goodness for that," I said. "I could use the rest." In fact, I was hoping to have another chance to visit with the baron's eldest daughter, Isabella. In that desire, however, I was to be thwarted, for we soon discovered that Isabella had departed for Oxford that very morning, returning to Somerville College for the Trinity Term.

As we approached the castle's main entrance at the far end of the drive, the young girl Rosie came dashing out to greet us.

"You're here at last!" she shouted gleefully. "We were getting worried."

"We?" the professor said.

"Me and Greymalkin. We'd begun to think that maybe the evil spirits out there on that island had dragged all of you into the otherworld and we'd never see you again."

"There are evil spirits on that island? *Now* you tell us," Challenger said.

"That's what I've heard. Probably just what they call an old wife's tale."

Lady Penhenthy and the baron welcomed us and invited us in. Then one of their servants led us up the staircase to the rooms we'd occupied previously.

"Will dinner in half an hour suit you?" she asked.

"Splendidly," replied the Reverend Mason.

I was the first one down. Rosie's sisters, Carmelita and Josella, shy and well-mannered young ladies, were in the drawing room, ostensibly to welcome their guests, though it was hard to get two words out of them. They obviously had quiet personalities, unlike their elder and younger sisters. Finally they informed me that Isabella had returned to Oxford that morning. They said she was disappointed that she wouldn't have a chance to see us before she had to leave. I didn't mention how great my own disappointment was.

Then Rosie waltzed into the drawing room followed by her cat, Greymalkin.

"The cat comes on little fog feet," I said.

Rosie gave me a startled look. She knitted her brows for a moment before crying out, "No, no, no. That isn't it at all."

"Goodness, Rosalinda," her mother said, coming in at that moment. "You must speak in a more lady-like voice to our guests."

"But he got it all wrong," she declared sternly. "What he said wasn't what the poet wrote."

"What did he write?" I asked.

" 'The fog comes on little cat feet,' not 'The cat comes on little fog feet.'"

"The fog has cat feet?" I asked.

"It's a metaphor," she asserted. "At least that's what Miss

Flowers calls it."

"I do believe she is correct," said my father-in-law, who'd come in just a moment earlier. "And I do believe, Ted, that you are teasing the girl."

"Well, perhaps so," I admitted, "but her cat does have little fog feet. Besides, that's a line written by an American poet. There's no telling what an American poet might come up with."

"That's what Miss Flowers says as well," Rosie remarked, "though she quite likes some of them, Longfellow especially."

Over dinner we regaled our hosts by recounting some of our adventures on Ynys Enlli, though careful to omit some of the more salacious bits.

Dr. Atkinson waxed eloquent about the company of monks who lived there—the chief monk named Anthony, the intellectual monk named Adelard, the gourmet monk named Aled, the gardener monk named Thomas, the pair of Irish monks, and finally the strange little jug-eared monk named Malachi who had a remarkable knack for predicting storms. Atkinson related little anecdotes about each of them, and for my liking he said a bit too much about how Malachi seemed to be especially taken by me.

McCauley Wilkins was emboldened enough to describe our precarious adventure in St. Mary's Tower. This was the first time my companions had heard the story, because neither McCauley nor I had spoken of it since it occurred.

McCauley credited me with having risked my own life to save his. It all made me quite uncomfortable, especially since I knew something about it that no one else knew, that I'd come close to letting him fall so that I wouldn't share his demise. But Wilkins's version made me out to be a hero.

Then my father-in-law spoke of the abundant wildlife on the island. He remarked on the great variety of sea birds before turning his attention to his particular favorites, the grey seals in their sanctuary cove.

When he described their cove, Rosie interrupted him by saying, "What do you call a group of grey seals in a cove?" She didn't give anyone time to respond before saying, "a coven of seals."

"Rosie has witches on the brain," Josella said.

"Actually, Rosie," Challenger said, "the answer to your riddle is, a choir of seals. But your suggestion of a coven of seals is quite clever."

"What I really want to know," the little girl asked, "is did Greymalkin's spell have any effect on Mr. Malone? Well, did it?" She crossed her arms across her chest and gave me a bold look.

"Rosie, don't be rude," said Lady Penhenthy.

"It's a fair question," I replied, "but I'm not entirely sure how to answer it. But Rosie, I need to tell you that when I was on the island I made friends with another cat, a totally white cat whose name was Gwynnie. She belonged to the monk Malachi, and like him, she was eager to befriend me.

Kindred spirits, one might say."

"Drat it!" Rosie blurted out. 'That white cat Gwynnie was probably a *good* witch. She must've put a counter-spell on you, one that canceled out Greymalkin's spell. Well, that explains it, anyway. Mr. Malone, you had some powerful friends out there on that island, friends who were looking out for you, didn't you? Almost like guardian angels."

"Yes, Rosie, I'm rather certain that I did."

After the evening meal we all moved into the castle's coziest room, which Lady Penhenthy called the music room. The three young women were eager to perform for us, and we were happy to provide them with a willing audience. We took seats on sofas and comfortable stuffed chairs, and as I gazed about the room, I saw a Broadwood piano placed close to the French doors, an open violin case lying behind a music stand, a large harp with an ornately carved wooden frame, and a silver flute. The three girls trooped in and placed themselves beside their instruments: Rosie was the flutist, Josella the harpist, and Carmelita the violinist. The piano bench remained empty; I assumed that was because Isabella was absent.

The young women needed a moment to tune and adjust their instruments, and when they were ready, Carmelita said in a loud, clear voice, "There's no need to tell you what this first piece is that we'll be playing. You'll all be quite familiar with it." Then they began playing "Green Sleeves," the flute and the violin playing the melodic line in unison, the chords of the harp providing a harmonious background. The girls were obviously accomplished musicians, and they gave the simple tune a haunting, almost ethereal sound.

"Superb," proclaimed Challenger, as we applauded roundly. "Do play some more!"

"This next one is called 'The Gypsies in the Glen'," Carmelita said, and they broke into a lively, jaunty dance tune I was unfamiliar with. It was a delightful piece, but it didn't cast the same spell on me that "Green Sleeves" had.

"And for our final song," Carmelita said, "'The Dance of the Fairies'." This tune started off with just Rosie on her flute, the opening notes high, wistful, and haunting; then Josella came in adding lush chords with the harp; and finally Carmelita's violin chimed in and slowly the tune's tempo began to grow more spritely. It made me think of the music I'd heard coming from the faerie mound on Ynys Enlli. Here, no drums, though the harp was filling that role, and here Rosie's flute was not as high pitched or as piercing to the ear as the piping had been at the mound. Nevertheless, their music took me back a couple of nights to my frightening but enthralling experience on the island. It brought to mind the siren-call to which I had nearly succumbed, and it caused me to lapse into a kind of reverie.

When they brought the piece to its conclusion, I sat there with my hands folded in my lap as my companions applauded loudly.

Rosie gave me a puzzled look. "You didn't care for it?" she asked in a soft voice.

Rousing myself from my stupor, I replied, " Oh, Rosie, it was so lovely that it cast a spell on me."

"Well, good," she said. "Perhaps casting a spell on you helps to make up for Greymalkin's spell that other dratted white cat Gwynnie managed to counteract."

As our hosts and my companions began leaving the room, I glanced back at the empty piano bench. For a second I pictured Isabella sitting there, her fingers arched above the keys. I wondered if I would ever see that appealing, intriguing young woman again.

41

It was a long, long day. We caught the early morning train from Bangor to Chester, where we transferred to the London train, which took us through Birmingham. Then, British Rail not failing us for once, we finally arrived at London's Euston Station a little before midnight. Each of us preferred doing it that way rather than breaking it into a two-day journey, as we'd done on the outward portion of our trip. We were all eager to get back to London and the comforts of our own habitations.

Conversation during the tedious train ride was kept to a minimum and what conversation did take place was desultory. We weren't yet ready or eager to be discussing and dissecting our experiences on Ynys Enlli. We would get to that in good time.

As the others napped or stared out the windows, I worked on my notes. At one point the Reverend Mason fired up his pipe, bringing a disgusted look from Dr. Atkinson, who left the carriage in favor of a walk through the train.

For most of the journey McCauley Wilkins sat huddled in his corner, though now the man seemed much less "the wee timorous sleeked beastie" he'd been during the initial phase of our journey. Of the six of us, to all outward appearances, he was the one most changed by our experiences on Ynys Enlli. If the Reverend Mason had set a specific goal for McCauley, it seemed to me that he might have achieved it.

Whether or not I would achieve my goal remained to be seen. I'd gone to the island in the hope of obtaining a good story for the newspaper, and I still had no doubt that a good story was there to be had. But for the life of me, I didn't know how to tell it. News stories were supposed to be based on facts and hard evidence. When we'd returned from the Lost World we had a fantastic story to tell, but we also had some spectacular evidence to back it up. What did I have this time? As far as I could tell, nothing more than impressions and suppositions. If that were all I had to base my story on, my editor, Mr. McCardle, would unleash his Scottish temper upon me with unthinkable (though not unimaginable) consequences.

As the train rumbled along through the gloom of evening, I couldn't help reflecting upon some of the most memorable events of the past few days, events that I knew required serious contemplation. Several of them I found amusing or endearing—such as my interactions with Rosie and her "witch-cat" Greymalkin; or the affinity the odd little monk named Malachi had felt for me. Then there was the sudden and genuine attraction I had felt for Rosie's eldest sister, Isabella, an attraction I'd had the foolish temerity to hope might be mutual. But other events remained thoroughly disconcerting. And I knew that two crucially important things had happened to me out there on the island were events that I would have to face up to and come to terms with—if I *could* come to terms with them.

42

During their long *day's journey into night, McCauley Wilkins sat in his corner seat in the railway car, his thoughts riffing through the major events of the last few days. In particular, he thought about the terrifying experience he'd had in the ruined church tower at the old abbey. He believed he was going to die, and he would have had not Ted Malone grabbed him and swung him to safety. It had been rather like a miracle. Like his guardian angel had been watching out for him and used Ted as the agent of his salvation.*

Only two weeks ago McCauley had stood alone on the Embankment in London staring down at the dirty water of the River Thames, willing himself to jump. He'd wanted to die but he'd been too cowardly to take his own life. But now he knew that he didn't want to die, that that was the lesson of his near-death experience in the church tower. And it was a lesson underscored by his May Eve experience at the Bardsey Apple Tree.

The events at the ancient apple tree were even more

inexplicable and more compelling than his near death in the tower. For through the agency of the tree, transformed into a physical manifestation of his deceased wife, he'd been offered the hope of a fresh beginning and given a reason to rejoice in the life he'd had and still did have. That was the meaning of May Day, and it had certainly taken on a fresh meaning for him. He and Felicity had had a kind of reconciliation, and it was clear that she had absolved him of any responsibility for her death.

McCauley recalled the conversation he and Ted Malone had had on the beach at Aberdaron on the night before they crossed to the island. It was a conversation about the Orpheus myth, and McCauley had wondered if he, like Orpheus, might have the courage to enter the Underworld and attempt to rescue his lost wife. Now, as he thought about what had occurred at the old apple tree, he realized that, in a way, he had experienced the Orpheus myth in reverse. He hadn't rescued Felicity. It was she who had rescued him. She had rescued him and then sent him back into the land of the living. But for her, as in the legend, there would be no return.

43

We were six exhausted, sleepy-eyed men as we gathered our belongings and exited the coach in London at Euston Station. My father-in-law and Dr. Atkinson climbed into a taxi that would take them to Victoria Gardens where they both had their residences. Wilkins and the Reverend Mason also shared a taxi, the two of them going to the financial district where they had flats. Lord John Roxton, in a third taxi, set off for Belgravia. I, alone, set off on foot. I had the shortest distance to go, since my current abode was in Bloomsbury, where I'd moved after Enid's death, not wanting to remain in the place where she and I had shared such happiness, albeit so briefly. My new flat was near Russell Square and the British Museum, and it was handy to my workplace at the newspaper office, being just a fifteen-minute walk through Holborn down to Fleet Street.

Wisps of fog clung to the air above Gower Street as I strode down the dark thoroughfare. The familiar darkness here in London was of a different quality to the darkness on Ynys Enlli. Here, too, there was rarely anything more than a faint glimmer of a starry sky. On the island, the night sky had been magical—at least, on the nights when it wasn't storming. The glorious night sky on May Eve would remain vividly in my mind forever. Still, I had a deep and abiding love for all things that meant London, and I knew that the dank coal-smoke laden fogs of London would always be dear to my heart.

I reached my little flat without incident, hardly seeing anyone else out on the streets at that hour. I was home again, after an adventure-filled two weeks, knowing I had experienced events I had to yet to process. But for now, I intended to do nothing more than sleep the sleep of the just.

"Well, Malone, you decided to come back and look in on us, did ya, lad? How thoughtful of you," Mr. McArdle said to me. "I certainly hope that after your little ghost-chasing jaunt you do be ready to be applyin' yor talents to some real work. I've saved up a goodly list of projects just for you, my lad, and I'd appreciate it if you were to hop to it, eh?"

For the next three weeks I hopped to it, not having any time to see my father-in-law or to think about the adventures we'd had on Ynys Enlli. That was probably a good thing. I needed a respite from thoughts of Ynys Enlli; and Professor Challenger and I, I felt, could both use a little break from each other. I rushed about in London Town doing the work of an earnest reporter for one of London's popular, though less august, daily newspapers, *The News Gazette*. It was exhausting work but it gave me real pleasure throwing myself into my menial tasks in a mindless fashion. I was much better off probing into the secret doings of others than probing into my own actions and thoughts.

"So these ghosties of yours," Mr. McCardle said to me one day in mid-June, "anything likely to come of that dafty business? You were a wee bit excited about that project before you set off for the wilds of Wales. Now, nary a word about it. So, what gives, eh Malone?"

"Not quite sure, sir. But it's still secure in the back of my mind. There's a lot there, but I've been having some difficulty figuring out how best to tell a tale that's so much based on speculation and suppositions rather than objective facts or evidence."

"Hmm. Why don't the two of us have a sit-down tomorrow morning and you can run through the whole thing for me. Maybe, if we put our pair of mickle brains together, we might figure something out. Don't want all your time and effort, not to mention the expenses, to come ta naught, you know."

44

As I climbed the stairs to Professor Challenger's third floor flat, I heard the footsteps of another person one flight above me. When I reached the landing outside my father-in-law's door, McCauley Wilkins stood there rapping on it. I arrived beside him just as Austin opened the door.

"Good evening gentlemen," my father-in-law's ancient manservant intoned. "The professor awaits you in the sitting room. Mr. Wilkins, may I take your hat?" Austin's glance at me was slightly tinged with disapproval, though by now he was familiar with the fact that I had an aversion to wearing hats. As he placed McCauley's hat on the hat stand, I noticed the three other hats already hanging there. Wilkins and I were obviously the last to arrive.

Austin ushered us into the sitting room where Dr. Nathaniel Atkinson, the Reverend J. M. Mason, and Lord John Roxton occupied well-upholstered chairs. James

Edward Challenger sat in his customary wing chair across from the fireplace looking every bit as formidable as ever. I had worried about the toll our arduous trip might have taken on him, but now his appearance suggested he had fully recovered from any deleterious effects. Indeed, it may have served to reinvigorate him.

We all exchanged warm greetings, and I found my thoughts returning to the night in this room when we'd had our initial discussion about psychic phenomena, the discussion that led us to embark on our pilgrimage to a place rumored to be rife with them. At that time, apart from my father-in-law and Lord Roxton, I hadn't known the other men. But now I did, and in general I quite liked them— even including the Reverend Mason, a man who, during our trip, had sometimes rubbed me the wrong way. Shared adventures have a habit of forging bonds even amongst the most disparate of fellows.

Austin served each of us with the drink we desired, whisky for Professor Challenger and Lord Roxton, glasses of claret for Mason and Wilkins, pints of bitter for Dr. Atkinson and me.

"Thank you, Austin," my father-in-law said. "We'll surely need additional refreshing before the evening's done."

"Indeed, sir," he said.

"Well, chaps," Professor Challenger said, "have we distanced ourselves sufficiently from our adventures on that little Edenic isle that we can now reflect back on them rationally and dispassionately?"

"Edenic?" Wilkins said, with raised eyebrows.

"He's being facetious, I would reckon," Lord Roxton said with a half-smile.

"Edenic if you're a seal," I said, "as rumor has it my father-in-law is, from time to time."

"Edenic," Mason grumped. "Good thing Brother Adelard didn't hear you make that crack. He would accuse you of blaspheming again."

"That fellah," Lord Roxton said, "learned as he was, sadly lacked a sense of humor. It's entirely too easy to bait such a fellah. Rather like shooting pedants in a barrel."

"Well, chaps," Challenger said, "I think it's high time we have a serious chat about what really happened to each of us out there on that far-flung isle. Why don't we take turns describing what each of us experienced? And why don't we focus particularly on what we experienced on May Day Eve?" Challenger looked about the circle at the faces of the others, and there were no demurs. "I'll happily lead off to get the ball rolling. Would that be all right?"

We made murmurs of assent, though it seemed to me that Mason and Wilkins were less enthusiastic about this proposal than the rest of us were.

"Well then, following our evening meal with the monks that night, I chose to spend the early hours of that evening down at the seal cove with my sleek-coated friends. They barked cheerful greetings to me, which I took as an invitation to regale them in song," Challenger said.

"So you sang to the seals?" I asked.

"I rather think he's giving himself the benefit of the doubt when he says he sang," Lord Roxton remarked.

"Quite right," Challenger replied, "to call my croaking singing is pushing it—not at all like those Welsh lads who sang so beautifully in the pub that night—though the seals seemed appreciative of my noble gesture, unlike some other folks I could name.

"Afterward I spread out a blanket which I'd brought with me and stretched out on the sand of the cove. I shut my eyes for a moment and drifted off into a gentle sleep. Then in my sleep a woman appeared before me. To all appearances she was my wife, Jessica, my wife as she had looked as a very young and desirable woman. Oh, dear me: '*Methought I saw my late espoused saint, brought to me, like Alcestis, from the grave,*'" he quoted. "Oh, how much I had missed her. I was ecstatic at seeing her again. My life had never been the same without my beloved Jessie. But then when she moved to kiss me, I knew something was amiss. For the first time, she had failed to say the words she always said before we kissed. Something wasn't right and so I rebuffed her. And in a sudden fit of pique, she—whoever or whatever she was— glared at me, called me a vile name, and then dissolved in a mist right before my very eyes."

"" *. . . as to embrace me she inclin'd, I wak'd, she fled, and day brought back my night,*'" I said, quoting the final words of Milton's sonnet.

"Yes, a rude awakening indeed. But the vile demonic creature had been tempting me, trying to steal my soul by sucking it forth with her kiss. I'd foiled her diabolical plan in the nick of time, but having first exulted at the sight of my dear Jessie, illusory though it was, and then having it suddenly taken away, that was a terrible wrench indeed."

We all remained silent at the conclusion of Challenger's words. His face told us how genuine his grief was. I thought I saw a tear glisten in the corner of one eye.

"No, that Edenic isle, like the Biblical Eden," he said, "was not free of malicious, malignant spirits. There were ghosts there and some of them were vile demons." Looking sad and wistful, he lifted his glass of whisky to his lips and sipped.

"Well, Ted," he said after a short pause, "how about you going next?" Reluctantly, I nodded my agreement.

So, I related my adventures at the fairy mound as well as I could. I described the music and the procession of the Fairy Folk and the light that radiated both from them and the opening in the mound. I told them of the young woman who'd beckoned to me, and I didn't shy away from admitting my intense desire to go with her and the other Fairy Folk when they urged me to. I confessed to having intense feelings of sadness and dejection after they were gone. I admitted that it was the touch of the hand of a woman I'd loved and a single spoken word from her that prevented me from doing so. I described the young creature's disappointment at my decision and how the golden circlet she'd held out to me with the glowing red gemstone had trickled down into the grass, its light fading away to nothing. I admitted that a keen longing to be with the Fairy Folk still remained in my heart.

"Do you think it was all real?" Dr. Atkinson asked me. "Or could it all have been some kind of strange hallucination? As I recall, you had had a goodly amount of that potent cider that evening, after several days of abstinence."

"I don't know," I admitted. "It's possible that it was all some sort of illusion. But I know that the pain in my heart is real."

"What do you think would have happened if you'd actually gone with the Fairy Folk?" Wilkins asked.

"Ted would have lived for three hundred years in Tir-na-nOg, the Land of the Ever Young, like Oisin did," Challenger said. "Until he missed all of us so much that he wanted to come back."

"And then when he stepped from the boat onto dry land," Lord Roxton added, "he would have turned into a handful of dust, since in the mortal world he would have been three hundred years old."

"I just wish I'd heeded Malachi's advice and not gone to that dratted fairy mound," I said. "What a fool I was. Fergus and Malachi both warned me against going there."

"I have a suspicion," Challenger said, "that Brother Malachi, all appearances to the contrary, was the wisest one from amongst that batch of mismatched monks."

"So, what about you, Mac?" my father-in-law said to McCauley Wilkins. "What's your tale of woe?"

Wilkins looked thoroughly disconcerted. "Umm . . . well . . . umm, I wandered off alone that evening and somehow, I wound up down there near that old apple tree. I settled down behind the barn, leaned my back against it, and before long I'd fallen asleep. Like you, professor, I dreamed of my wife." He paused for a moment as if lost in thought. "In my dream," he finally continued, "my deceased wife spoke kindly to me. She reminded me of all the good times we had once had together, and then she told me she knew I wasn't responsible for her death. She said the responsibility was solely hers, the result of her own foolish actions. We had a kind of reconciliation, I suppose, and for me the experience was a huge relief, since I had assumed that my action or inaction had contributed somehow to her terrible death. Her words of exoneration did wonders to assuage the oppression caused by my feelings of guilt."

He paused again to collect his thoughts. "Anyway, I guess for me my experiences that night were far more positive and more uplifting than the ones Ted or Professor Challenger had."

I'm not sure why, but I had a sense that Wilkins was holding something back, that he had glossed over his adventures and had chosen to omit some important things from his account. My father-in-law must have had the same feeling because he said, "That's it? Not very detailed, Mac.

Isn't there more you would like to add?"

"I fell asleep after that, and when I awoke, you and Ted were sitting alongside me."

"That old apple tree had a strange, almost magical, allure that night," Challenger said. "You and me and Ted, we were all drawn to it as if we had no choice."

"I felt it, too, said Dr. Atkinson, "though I was otherwise detained."

"Do go on, Nathaniel," urged the professor. The look on Wilkins's face told me he was relieved to be off the hot seat. I wondered if he might have skipped over some of the stranger parts of his experience.

"Well," Dr. Atkinson said, "I must confess that that evening I turned into something of a voyeur."

"My word," said the reverend.

"After our evening meal, as you'll recall, we each of us pretty much went our own separate way. Mason and Wilkins went along with a few of the monks to their religious service. You, Professor, wandered off in the direction of your seal cove, Lord John went I know not where, and Ted was meandering about in the monks' graveyard. As for me, I decided I had better take advantage of the pleasant dry evening to climb the old church tower. It was a perfect evening for viewing the great peaks of Snowdonia, something I much wished to do. It was a bit tricky navigating all those worn old steps, but my goodness it was well worth it. What a splendid view from atop that tower. I must have remained there for nearly half an hour luxuriating in the sight of that glorious panorama.

"When I turned my gaze to nearby events, that's when I saw Ted down amongst the tombstones. I watched him as he chatted with the odd little monk named Malachi, who whose faithful companion that evening appeared to be a fluffy white cat. Malachi hadn't attended the service, nor had Brother Thomas. I spotted him poking about in his terraced garden higher up the slope. Then farther up the slope I caught sight of Brother Fergus and Brother Liam. They were climbing up the trail that leads to the peak at the top of Bardsey Mountain. As I took a hard look up at the mountain peak, it seemed to me there was a cairn or perhaps some kind of ancient shrine up there. When the pair of monks got to the top, they kindled a fire upon the shrine. It appeared to me they were performing a ritual of some kind. Was it a Christian ritual? Or was it some kind of rite or ceremony I wasn't familiar with, perhaps a pagan rite of some kind?" He glanced about at the blank faces of the other men.

"Before I climbed down from the tower, the service in the chapel had ended, and I watched Mason and Wilkins as they began making their way back in the direction of the hostel. Dark was just beginning to fall, so I decided I'd best get myself safely back down those treacherous steps and make my own way toward the hostel.

"Anyway, I'd spent all that time watching the doings of others. But as for me, I can't admit to having had any extraordinary or supernatural events that involved specters, phantoms, or apparitions, unlike my compatriots seem to have had. That night I came up empty.

"But despite that, I must say that I don't for a moment doubt that my compatriots did have the experiences they've described, whether illusory or not. I am entirely convinced that that island we visited is indeed a repository of immense psychic energy, an energy that at certain times erupts into remarkable and powerful manifestations, as it did to others, though not to me.

"But what about the night of the great succubae infestation?" Challenger asked. "You shared in that event, as I recall."

"I did, sir. A most unusual and disarming event. It was like nothing I'd ever heard of before, every one of us sharing the experience at the same time. Wondrous strange."

"Not everyone of us," Mason countered grumpily, "but most of you, it seems."

"So you missed out?" Lord Roxton said. "What a shame. Might have done you some good."

"Har," shot back the Reverend Mason.

"Are you grumpy because you were left out of the fun?" my father-in-law said. "Or is that just your normal disposition?"

Mason, his eyes narrowed and his lips compressed with displeasure, offered no reply.

"Don't take offense, my dear sir," Challenger said, "we're only twitting you."

"Oh yes, that's what I assumed," Mason replied, his arms crossed upon his chest."

"If those monks up on the mountaintop were performing a pagan ritual," I said, "it was surely connected with the fact that it was May Day Eve."

"Of course," Dr. Atkinson said. "And I suspect that's also why several of the monks chose not to attend the church service that evening," Dr. Atkinson said. "They were answering a different call."

"And it was surely due to it's being May Eve that several of us had our strange encounters with the spirit realm that night," Challenger opined. "It was that one night in the year, more than all the others, when such things were prone to occur."

"That does seem to be the case," Dr. Atkinson agreed, "though All Hallows Eve may be a similar occasion. The exceptional powers of the spirit world on that one night might help to account for the fact that no Christian feast day was ever superimposed upon May Day, as I do believe we have previously discussed."

"I don't understand," Wilkins said. "Wouldn't they want to do that even more if it was a time when pagan spirits were loosed upon the world?"

"Not if they preferred to leave well enough alone, not tempt fate, as it were," Challenger said.

"I still don't understand," Wilkins said.

"What he's suggesting," Mason said, "is that the early

Christian fathers were aware of there being extraordinary potency to the pagan spirits at that particular time, and so they chose not to engage them or rile them. I find such a suggestion heretical and unworthy of my learned friends."

"It's merely a suggestion, my dear sir," Challenger said. "Don't take it as a personal affront to your faith."

"Well, I do."

"If the Christian saints prevail over the pagan deities the vast majority of days and nights during the year, as I believe we all agree they do, can't we allow them to be in their full glory for just one or two nights?" Dr. Atkinson said.

I'd noticed that Lord John Roxton, usually eager to add fuel to the fire, was steering clear of this contestation. He sat there quietly with his hands in his jacket pockets, a hint of a smile on his lips. Lord John was a wise man.

"Wilkins?" Challenger asked. "Any opinion from your direction?"

"Uh, no, not really, sir. But I guess I would opt for what I remember the reverend saying once before, that the sense of hopefulness and fresh beginning signified by May Day is pretty much the same for Christians and non-Christians. Therefore, there's no need for a special Christian holy day at the beginning of May to balance off the pagan spirits."

Professor Challenger ran his hand through his thick, salt and pepper beard, then said, "Well put, my dear sir, well put." The Reverend Mason, too, beamed a smile at his friend.

Our confab continued for another hour or so, and then

the others began to leave. As I often did, I remained behind to have a few additional minutes with my father-in-law, who in recent years had become my closest friend and confidant.

As I was preparing to leave also, he looked at me with a twinkle in his eye and said, "Ted, on that morning when we were about to depart from the island, I believe that Brother Malachi, as he was placing those scallop shells around our necks, slipped something else into your hand. You've never said anything about that. I was wondering if it might have been something connected with events on that fateful evening. Is that a possibility?"

I hadn't realized he'd spotted Malachi slipping the little pouch into my hand, but I guess I shouldn't have been surprised. It's never easy to put anything over on Professor George Edward Challenger. And, obviously, he very much wanted to know what Malachi had given me.

I felt my right trousers pocket, knowing that the pouch was there. "Is it possible that it had something to do with the fateful evening?" I said, repeating my father-in-law's question. "Well, yes, I suppose it is possible."

Slowly I extracted the cloth pouch from my pocket, loosened the drawstring that held it closed, and then tipped out a small solid object into my father-in-law's open palm.

"My word!" he exclaimed as he stared down at the glowing red gemstone.

45

With a solid night's sleep under my belt, I was up early, eager to greet the day. The morning had broken clear and bright, and a chorus of songbirds extemporized gleefully outside my flat's bedroom window. The congenial company and lively conversation at last night's gathering had been just what I'd needed to buoy my spirits, and now, it seemed to me, the lusty singing of the birds on this bright June day was a propitious sign—summer had come to London.

I had a bounce in my step as I strolled through Holborn on my fifteen-minute walk to *The News Gazette*, my place of employment. As I often did, I I felt my right trouser pocket for the little pouch containing a small red gemstone. I couldn't be certain, but I suspected the gemstone was the one that sat atop the golden circlet the young woman had held out to me. When I rebuffed her, the circlet lost its luminescence, and she dropped it down into the tall grasses near the fairy mound. Maybe the stone came loose and Brother Malachi stumbled upon it and saved it for me. Anyway, the stone in my pocket was one he'd given to me, and ever since I had kept it close as if it were a lucky talisman.

I strode down South Hampton Row for a ways, then cut over to Chancery Lane and stepped jauntily on down to Fleet Street. My blood was circulating and my brain cells were sparking. I smiled and nodded at perfect strangers whom I met along the way, sometimes receiving smiles and nods in return, sometimes startled looks. I felt like a new man—or at least like a *renewed* man. And suddenly I had an epiphany. What was causing me to feel so good, I realized, was the simple fact of being in London, the place I most wanted to be. I was *not* off in some mystical dreamland, *not* off with those Celtic faerie folk in their splendiferous otherworld. The desires I had had on May Eve, I realized, had been just a momentary whimsy, a strange psychological aberration induced by the seductive allure of their music and their physical beauty. Those luminous creatures had placed their spell on me; they'd tried to entice me away from the mortal realm and had nearly succeeded. But they *hadn't*. Enid, my dear, dear Enid, advised me otherwise, and I had been wise enough to follow her advice. I would always be grateful to her. And now at last, here in my beloved city, I was entirely free from those creatures' spell. Now I no longer felt tormented by the thought that I should have gone with them. Those feelings no longer existed. I was here in the normal mortal world, here where I belonged: here in London Town.

On this bright June morning the sights and sounds of the city thrilled my senses. Not too far off ahead of me I could see the splendid tower of the church of St. Dunstan-in-the-West. And maybe a quarter of a mile off to my left, high above the rooftops of the surrounding buildings, rose the great dome of St. Paul's Cathedral. There was nothing in the faerie otherworld half as magnificent as that! Enid had saved me that night, and this morning the wonders of my London now completed my reclamation. Now I was entirely free of the faeric folk's fatal allure. But what I still had yet to do was come up with a way to relate the tale of our adventures on Ynys Enlli, relate them in a way that would please our readers and that would pass muster with the critical eye of my hardnosed editor, Mr. McArdle.

Last night, as I was in a state halfway between waking and sleeping, the first hint of how I might tell the story of our adventures on Ynys Enlli began slowly to creep into my brain. Now, as I strode along the familiar streets of the city, that idea had morphed into a firmer shape. I liked it. But whether I could sell Mr. McArdle on it, that was another matter entirely.

At Temple Bar, I swung left onto Fleet Street and walked quickly past all the law courts and law offices. It was too early in the day for many barristers or solicitors to be out and about, but a bit farther along Fleet Street there were more signs of life around the offices of our rival newspapers. Finally I came within sight of the old brick building that housed *The News Gazette,* a decrepit edifice probably erected sometime early in the previous century.

As I entered I could hear the ground floor presses clacking away. I breathed in the smell of newspapers being printed and saw the workers trundling crates of freshly printed newspapers out to the loading dock at the rear of the building.

Still feeling energized, I bounded up the two flights of stairs to where the main newsroom was located, then strode down the center aisle between the mostly unoccupied desks to the chief editor's office at the far end of the room. The door to Mr. McArdle's office was open indicating that he was in. This morning he must've arrived earlier than usual, for I normally got there half an hour ahead of him.

I'd worked up my nerve to float my proposal to him first thing, not knowing what his response might be. Better to broach the matter right off and get it over with. As I came in, he rose from behind his desk, a scowl on his face.

"So Malone," he said, "about those auld Welsh ghosties of yours, you been givin' some thought to how you might be tackling the matter?"

"Well, yes sir, just a bit. And I wanted to get your opinion of what I've been thinking."

"Hmm. Well, laddie, I been giving 'em a bit of thought too, and let me tell you the suggestion I have to make to you. What would you be thinkin' of this? I were a-thinkin' that if you cannae spin this tale of yours like a proper news story, then how about trying to tell it as a spritely work of fiction. Perhaps you could spin it into an exciting yarn, something our readers might take to. If you think you could, then maybe we could run it in installments, like they did last century with auld Dickens and Wilkie Collins and some o' the others I cannae think of at the moment. We could ballyhoo it as a return to the kind o' yarns that once stirred readers up. It'd be quite a change of pace for us, but it might just stir up some fresh interest in this dusty old rag of ours. Goodness knows, we need it. So, what do you think of that, laddie?"

What Mr. McArdle was suggesting was exactly what I'd been about to propose to him. But I quickly chose not to mention that fact. Better if he thought the idea was uniquely his own. If it had come from me, there was a good chance he would have scotched it.

I rubbed my chin as if deep in thought. "Hmm," I said at last. "What an intriguing notion. But, yes, maybe I could just pull it off. I like it your suggestion, sir, like it a lot."

"Oh, and laddie, here's something else that might please you. We've just hired a bonnie lass who I want to be assisting you—well, not hired exactly. She's an unpaid summer volunteer, just come up to London from one of them women's colleges at Oxford. She's a real gem, my lad, a real gem. Ah, here she comes now."

I swung about to watch as the "bonnie lass" moved down the central aisle of the newsroom towards us. She was a bonnie lass indeed, tallish, with wavy chestnut-colored hair that fell to her shoulders. She was a lass with an extremely lovely smile.

"Miss, I'd like you meet a fella who considers himself my ace reporter, Mr. Edward Malone."

"Why, Mr. McArdle," she said in a voice I remembered, "I believe I've met Mr. Malone. Sir," she said, looking at me and extending one hand, "it's a pleasure to see you again. I believe we shall enjoy working together."

Then, for just a brief moment, I imagined the soft touch of a hand on my shoulder. And then I imagined hearing a low voice say, "Yes, Ted, she's the one. She is truly a gem." Maybe it wasn't all just my imagination.

My morning had gotten off to a grand beginning. And in the last minute or two, my day had become even grander than it had been before.

Acknowledgments

I am deeply grateful to my writing compatriots in Williamsburg—Kathleen Jabs, Sally Stiles, Len Shartzer, and Jim Tobin—for their many suggestions and invaluable criticisms. I am also especially grateful to Anna Branscome, Cory Ragsdale, and my brother, Roger L. Conlee, for their careful reading of the manuscript. The errors that remain are entirely mine.

Sir Arthur Conan Doyle's Professor Challenger tales provided the impetus for this short novel. Those tales, never among the most popular of Doyle's works, are of uneven quality. None of them rise to the level achieved by a writer such as H. G. Wells, with the exception of Doyle's *The Lost World,* which stacks up well with the best early science fiction/fantasy novels.

— John Conlee